Jane and the Chalet School

The Chalet School series by Elinor M. Brent-Dyer

This is a complete list of Chalet School titles in chronological order. Those titles printed in bold type have been published in paperback in Armada but not all are currently available. Please send a sae to the Marketing Department, Collins Children's Division, for an up-to-date stocklist.

Elinor M. Brent-Dyer

Jane
and the
Chalet School

To Sidney

First published in Great Britain in 1964
by W. & R. Chambers Ltd, Edinburgh
First published in Armada in 1990
This impression 1991

Armada is an imprint of
the Children's Division, part of
HarperCollins Publishers Ltd,
77–85 Fulham Palace Road,
Hammersmith, London W6 8JB

Printed and bound in Great Britain by
HarperCollins Manufacturing, Glasgow

Contents

CHAPTER 1

Enter – Jane

Jack Lambert was in a tearing rage. She stumped along the corridor from Matron's room, her mouth a straight line, her black eyes sparkling with a reddish light, even her boy's crop of straight hair crisping with her fury.

"What's biting her?" demanded Barbera Hewlett, prefect of Lower IVʙ, the form both she and Jack adorned. "She *can't* have got in a row already? We haven't been back at school for more than two minutes."

"But ask her, my Barbara," advised Corinne Sambeau, another member of the form. "Then you will know, n'est-ce pas?"

"Ask her yourself!" Barbara retorted. "She might just as well bite you as me."

Corinne laughed. "But not me, I do not wish une brouille. Sans doute, c'est mieux que l'on ne dit rien."

"How true! Say nothing it is," Barbara assented. "Come on, Corinne! We'd better unpack our nightcases before Matey arrives."

They moved off to their dormitory, known as Violet from its violet-besprinkled curtains and rugs. There, they found that a minor change had taken place. Meg Walton, who had been there the whole year so far, was busied in removing her various possessions from her cubicle. As the pair entered she was piling photos and a couple of story-books on top of the garments already heaped on the light wickerwork tray which her particular chum, Angela Carton, was helping her to fill.

"Jumping Jemima! What's happened?" Barbara cried. "You surely aren't deserting us, Meg? Who says, anyhow?"

"Matey," Meg said, burrowing under the bed for the red velvet tomato which was her pincushion. "She grabbed me the moment I got here and told me I was to move into Alpenrose for this term and Jack Lambert was coming here in my place – *got* him!" She came up with the tomato and grinned at Barbara and Corinne. "Sooner you than me! Jack'll have heaps to say about being moved out of Len Maynard's dormy. She won't be able to latch on to her so easily for answers to all her questions."

"But why?" Barbara demanded.

"Don't ask me – I wouldn't know. That's the last, Angel. Come on! We'd better get a move on."

The pair seized the handles at either end of the tray and prepared to march off with it, leaving the other two gaping. It was not usual at the Chalet School for girls to be moved from one dormitory to another during the year unless there was a good reason for it and, as Barbara had said, there hadn't been time so far for either Meg or Jack to provide such a reason, seeing term had just begun.

Before anyone could say anything the door was flung open and Jack stalked in, her arms full of coats and dresses. Two more of the occupants of Pansy followed her with the usual tray, laden with her other belongings. One look at her face warned the girls to say nothing. She came to a full stop and glared round at them.

"Where am I to go?" she demanded.

"In here," Meg replied. "At least that's what Matey told me. I've cleared so you can unpack at once. Come on, Angel! I don't want to be all night over it!"

The pair departed and Jack stamped into the cubicle, tossing her armful on the bed. Wanda von Eschenau and

Renata van Buren came with the tray which they set on the floor.

"O.K. That's all," Jack said briefly. "You can scram. Ta!"

They went and she promptly pulled the cubicle curtains close with a vim that set the rings jangling. A dead silence followed, broken only by a thud as Jack pulled out a drawer so violently that it landed on the floor with a crash.

"Has it hurt you?" Barbara cried involuntarily.

"No – ta," was all Jack vouchsafed.

"May we, perhaps, assist you?" Corinne hazarded.

"No – and leave me alone!"

The door opened and the dormitory prefect came in. Most folk liked Priscilla Dawbarn, but her pleasant welcome to Jack was met with a growled, "Thanks, but I didn't want to come."

"You'll like it once you've settled down," Priscilla said briskly. "Corinne – Barbara! Give Jack a hand, please."

"Don't want them!" came from behind the curtains.

"Oh, don't be so silly!" Priscilla said, distinct amusement in her voice. "You don't want to be up here all night, even if Matey allowed it. Come on, Jack! We'll soon have you settled." She opened the curtains and walked in, only just suppressing an exclamation of horror at sight of the muddle. "We'll hang up your coats and frocks first. That'll clear the bed. Here you are, Barbara. Hang those things up on Meg's old pegs. Corinne, you see to the shoes, will you? Now, Jack, blouses first. Oh, heavens! You *have* crumpled them! Lay them in as straight as you can."

Jack glowered at her. "Look here! I daresay you mean to be awfully decent and all that, but you may as well know first as last that I *loathe* being in this dormy and I couldn't care less what my things look like."

"No; but Matey will and she won't let you forget it," Priscilla said shrewdly, passing over Jack's decidedly rude manner.

"No; and I jolly well shan't let this blinking new kid that's been shoved into my cubey forget it either!" Jack burst out.

"Fiddle! It's not her fault you've been moved!" Priscilla retorted. "Blame Matey if you must blame someone."

"That's all *you* know! They've given her my cubey because her ma said it was the first time she'd been away from any of them and she might be unhappy at first and could she be in a dormy with someone who would help her out. So now!"

"Who told you that?" demanded Barbara who had come back in time to overhear this diatribe.

"Matey said so."

"Said it to *you*?" Priscilla asked, startled.

Jack reddened. "Not to me exactly. She was talking to Deney and I heard her. Oh, I wasn't *listening*, if that's what you're thinking. I'd banged once on the door so they knew I was there – or someone, at any rate. I banged again after that and they stopped talking and Matey told me about it – coming here, I mean."

"Then it's just as I said. Matey's the person to blame and not this new girl. So I hope you'll just let her alone, Jack. It would be jolly unfair if you took it out on her when she can't help it," Priscilla said severely. "Now stop blethering and let's get this mess cleared up. Corinne, half her hankies are falling out of the case; put them back, please. Roll up those stockings, Barbara. Hand me your blouses, Jack. Now be quick, all of you!"

Between them, they got the confusion cleared and the

cubicle restored to the immaculate neatness of the others. Priscilla marched them off downstairs and saw them into their common room before she went on to senior common room to unload the latest happenings on her own circle. Jack, meanwhile, stalked off to a corner where she hitched up a chair with her foot and sat down to gloom. As for the other two, they couldn't pour out their story fast enough. They were speedily the centre of an excited throng, all exclaiming at the news.

Into the general hubbub came the sound of the door opening and Miss Dene, the Head's secretary, entered with the new girl. The noise stopped at once. All eyes were fixed on the newcomer as Miss Dene introduced her.

"Girls! This is Jane Carew. She has come at the last moment and hasn't done the entrance exam yet, so we can't be sure which form she'll be in – one of the Lower Fourths, though, I expect. Someone – " her eyes roved over them and settled on Jack, "yes, you, Jack – look after her, please."

Miss Dene was a pleasant person, but she had her limits and not even in her present mood did Jack dare to disobey her. She came across the room unwillingly.

"Here you are, Jane!" Miss Dene said cheerfully. "This is Jack Lambert. She'll look after you and tell you everything you want to know. You're the same age so I expect you'll be in the same form. Fourteen in August, isn't it, Jack? And Jane was fourteen last week." She gave them a smile and departed and Jack was left in a quandary.

The new girl, with no idea of the wheels within wheels, came forward smiling, her hands held out. "Oh, darling!" she cried, "will you really give me a hand? It's too, too sweet of you! School's quite new to me, you know, though I've been dying for it for ages. Now do begin and tell me everything!"

There was a universal gasp from all but Jack. She stood, feet astride, hands in blazer pockets, glowering at the girl who, to her mind, had usurped her cubicle. The smile died out of Jane's face. No one could mistake the enmity blazing from Jack's eyes and Jane was ultra-sensitive to atmosphere. Her hands dropped and she looked anxiously round all of them.

No one spoke for a minute. The job was Jack's and they all knew the unwritten law of the school that new girls were to be looked after until they could feel their feet. Finally, Jack herself spoke.

"Not much use *my* telling you anything! You'll probably be in Upper IVB and I'm in a Lower A," she growled. "Anyhow, I can't be bothered with you. Someone else can see to you. I've *had* you!"

"But – I don't understand – " Jane began.

Jack interrupted her. "Don't you? Then I'll tell you so much. Because of you, I've been turfed out of my proper dormy where I've been ever since I came to school. Now!"

Jane looked bewildered. "But I *still* don't understand. I only went where the Matron told me. I hadn't a thing to do with it – honestly I hadn't! Oh, darling, you *must* see that!"

"Stop calling me 'darling' and *slobbering* over me!" Jack retorted. "We've no use for soppiness here, I can tell you!" She swung round, turning her back on Jane, who looked stunned. "Wanda – Gillie – Arda – all the lot of you – come on with me! I want you!"

Ignoring Jane completely, she marched out of the room, followed by the gang of which she was the leader. Jane looked after them, her lips quivering. Then she seemed to get hold of herself. Turning to the rest who had been too startled by Jack's behaviour to say or do anything, she said, "How *too* frustrating for her! Oh, I *am* sorry about it, but I hadn't a thing to do with it. Please believe that and do, someone, tell me a little of what I want to know."

José Helston, a slim fourteen-year-old from Upper IVB, came forward at once. "Of course we will! And don't worry about Jack. She'll snap out of it sooner or later. You see," she went on, "Len Maynard is dormy prefect for Pansy and Jack has latched on to her ever since she came – Jack I mean.[1] That's the why of all this. Come and sit over here, Jane, and we'll do what we can for you.

"Only," put in another girl, "we must make it plain to you that Jack is not foolish – what you call 'soppy' – about Len. In this school, we do not like such things. But Jack asks many questions and Len can answer them. If they are in different dormies, it will be difficult for Jack, you understand."

"Don't you believe it!" José broke in. "Jack will manage somehow, Adrienne. Trust her! Come and sit on the settee, Jane, and we'll help you all we can."

Jane went with them, but her deep grey eyes still held a hurt look which not all the friendliness of Upper IVB could dispel just then. And they *were* friendly in their efforts to make up for Jack's uncalled-for rudeness. They explained rules to her and answered all her queries. At the same time, there were quite a few questions they would have liked to ask themselves. Why, for instance, had Jane come to school in the summer term when the school year was almost ended? Why hadn't she been at school before? Why had she been given Jack's cubicle? Even the authorities knew about the odd friendship that existed between Len Maynard and Jack Lambert and it

[1] *Leader in the Chalet School.*

wasn't like them to make such a change without very good reasons. Quite a few other ideas came to them, but for the moment, they let those slide.

They explained that the School wad divided into four age-groups – Senior, Senior Middles, Lower Middles and Juniors. Upper IVB was bottom of the Senior Middles and Lower IVA was head of the Junior Middles. There were nineteen prefects, including the Head Girl, six of them being sub-prefects. They told her that the school not only played tennis and cricket in summer, but also, as soon as the weather was fit, they spent three afternoons a week down at Lake Thun for swimming and boating.

There was no time for much more. Bed came early for everyone on the first night of term, since most of them had had lengthy journeys that day. However, by the time they had to go upstairs, the members of Upper IVB had decided that there was a good deal that was very likeable about the new girl. She had a gay, eager manner that appealed to them; she certainly had a sense of humour and she wasn't sulky. They could all see that Jack's bitter enmity had hurt her but she had said nothing about it, giving her full attention to all they were telling her. She was attractive as well, with her dark grey eyes, ash-blond hair brushed straight back from her face into a pony-tail the ends of which turned into tiny ringlets, and clear, pale skin. She had a sweet voice and very clear enunciation and altogether she struck them as being quite a desirable member of form.

"Yes, I like her," José Helston told the other members of Marguérite when they were undressing. "I hope she comes to our form. Of course," she added as she laid down her brush and tied up her own long brown curls for the night, "we'll have to do something about her *language*."

14

"But how?" Adrienne Didier queried. "I find that she speaks very well and I like her voice."

"I didn't mean that, idiot! She's a lot too gushing – which is partly what's set Jack against her, I'll bet!" José said shrewdly.

"Don't you believe it!" Jean Abbot, the form prefect, took a hand. "It's being chucked out of Pansy to make room for her that's got Jack's goat. No; I *don't* mean that Jack's all gooey about Len. Don't be so daft, Thérèse! The thing is, Jack's always rather looked on Len as considerably much *her* possession. She'd loathe *anyone* who did that for her. And goodness knows how she'll get her questions answered now. You don't see much of a prefect – unofficially, I mean – unless you *are* in her dormy."

"That's true," Dilys Edwards agreed. "Where's she gone – Violet, isn't it? That's Pris Dawbarn. Well, no-one ever said that Pris was a – a prodigy of learning – "

"A *what*?" they chorused.

"A prodigy of learning," Dilys repeated serenely. "It's what my great-uncle from America said when he came to visit us these last hols. 'Well, great-niece, I guess this school of yours will be turning you into a real prodigy of learning!' Silly old ass!"

"I hope you said it wasn't," Sally Godfrey told her severely. "It sounds simply ghastly!"

"What do you take me for? And there's first bell! Me for bed!"

It was a case of all for bed. The second bell would ring five minutes later and anyone still up after that would have to finish undressing in the dark. The subject dropped and was temporarily forgotten in the wild scramble to get between the sheets before the duty prefect arrived to switch off the lights.

CHAPTER 2

Explaining Jane

If Upper IVB hoped to number Jane Carew among themselves, they were not the only ones to do so. Jane herself, having learned from their chatter that Jack Lambert was a member of Lower IVA, devoutly hoped that she would be good enough for the Upper form. Why Jack should so dislike her the moment they had set eyes on each other was something the new girl found hard to solve. It was hard luck on Jack to be parted from her mentor, but after all, Jane thought, it couldn't be so very difficult for her to ask Len Maynard her questions some time during the day; and everyone else concerned seemed to be positive that there was no question of silliness where the two were concerned.

"I'm a complete stranger to Jack," Jane pondered that first night as she lay staring into the darkness long after everyone else was asleep. "I hadn't anything to do with her being moved out of here. I just went where I was told. So why should she hate me so badly?"

Another idea came to her. "And what *did* she mean by saying I 'slobbered'? I'm sure I don't. And I'm certain I'm not 'soppy', whatever that may mean. If it's what I think it is, I'm definitely not. Mother and Father would never have stood for it. I do see that it must be very frustrating for her to be moved like this, but that's no reason for her to give me dirty looks and be so very – well – *beastly* to me!"

It was a puzzle she was unable to solve just then, so it

was as well that sleep swept down on her at that point – sleep so deep that she didn't even dream. And next morning, she had too much else to fill her mind to trouble about it.

The day before had been wet and gloomy, but the school woke to a lovely spring day – and to a spring day in Switzerland. Jane, tumbling out of bed to gaze out of the window, had all she could do to dress in time. She had travelled widely for a girl of her age, but never, she thought, as she stood brushing her hair and feasting her eyes on the scene outside, had she seen anything more lovely.

She was staring across a broad grassy shelf which ended in a cliff that fell steeply down to the valley far below. Beyond rose the snow-crowned glory of the Alps, rank on rank. Through the open window, the breeze came sweet with the scent of the early flowers. Jane's sensitive nostrils quivered as she drew it in. Her eyes shone.

"Oh, lovely – lovely – *lovely*!" she murmured to herself. "Oh, I *am* glad they sent me to school here! I'm going to love it, I know!"

It was just as well that she had those minutes of rapture, for with the beginning of school came the first of her troubles. While the others were hard at work unpacking, she was installed in the office where Miss Dene could keep an eye on her, and set to work on the entrance papers she had not yet done. Some of them she found easy enough, but she met her Waterloo over maths and science. The result was trouble for the staff when they came to discuss her.

"Her modern languages are excellent," Mlle de Lachennais, head of that department, reported. "She both speaks and reads fluently and grammatically and she has

17

a charming accent. But, hélas! of Latin she knows nothing
– but nothing at all!"

"I've no complaint to make about her English subjects," Miss Derwent, head of the English branch,
remarked. "She is extremely well-read for her age. Her
essay shows imagination, a real power of self-expression
and excellent choice of language. She's a little too fond
of adjectives and especially superlatives, but that's something she can be drilled out of. Nancy, what have you to
say about her maths?"

Nancy Wilmot laughed. "A complete headache, my
dear! She's quite good as far as she's gone in arithmetic.
Whoever taught her has made her set out her work clearly
and neatly. There, she can work with Upper IVB easily.
Waste of time to send her to Lower IVA. She'd make
rings round that crowd all the time. But, my dears, she
has just begun algebra and her geometry is exactly nil!"
She stopped with a grimace.

"*One* side of her history is good," Miss Charlesworth
took her turn. "What she knows, she knows thoroughly
and that includes dates, for a wonder. But she knows
nothing at all about constitutional and what you might
call commercial history and she's never been taught to
reason from cause to event."

It was the same with all other subjects. Except for
English, Jane's reports all contained a "but". Where she
was good, they all agreed that she could work with Upper
IVB. Where she was not, she was either at Lower IVA's
standard or even beneath it.

"She's a real pain in the neck!" sighed Miss Ferrars,
who was responsible for all junior geography and maths.

"Why is she so uneven?" Miss Yolland, the art mistress
and, like a good many of them, an Old Girl of the school,
asked with interest.

"Goodness knows! She only came at the last minute," Miss Derwent replied. "Where's Rosalie? She should be able to explain her."

"I'm here," said a quiet voice from the doorway.

With one accord, the mistresses swung round to greet the newcomer.

"You come here, Rosalie, and give us the gen on this new girl – Jane Carew!" Nancy Wilmot commanded. "Anyway, why come this term at all? It isn't done as a rule. Why not wait for the beginning of the new school year?"

Rosalie Dene laughed. "I guessed someone would ask that. There wasn't any help for it, my child."

"Why not?" Miss Derwent asked.

"Well, as far as the Carews were concerned, everything seemed to happen at once."

Miss Ferrars sat up. "Wait a moment – the Carews! That rings a bell! Rosalie Dene! Do you mean to say that this kid is the child of Sir William Carew – the man who tours Shakespeare and Sheridan and so on all over the world?"

Miss Dene nodded. "That's who she is."

"Then that explains her knowledge of Shakespeare," Miss Derwent said with decision. "I was rather startled. One doesn't expect such wide information as she displays at her age. But of course she must have been soaked in all that sort of thing from her cradle."

"But even that doesn't explain why she's so uneven," Miss Yolland pointed out. "Surely they packed her off to school as soon as she was old enough? You don't cart girls about with you as a rule – or do you?" she added.

"No; I imagine most stage folk do, as you say, pack their offspring off to boarding-school as soon as they're old enough," Rosalie agreed. "In this case, however, there were special circumstances."

"Such as what?" demanded Miss Armitage, whose subject was science and who had already been informed that Jane Carew knew no science whatsoever.

Rosalie perched on the nearest table. "It's quite a story. I'll be as brief as I can just now, though. Jane herself has always been an only child; but the year before she was born, the twin brother and sister who had preceded her by six years died in a 'flu epidemic in their school."

"But what a tragedy!" Mlle exclaimed. "The poor parents!"

Rosalie nodded. "It was pneumonic 'flu and very bad. One mistress and five of the children died, the Carew twins among them. Lady Carew was unable to get to them in time. The Company was touring the Middle West States of America and by the time they had the cable telling them of the epidemic, it was all over. The twins had gone."

"How ghastly!" Nancy Wilmot spoke soberly. "It must have been a horrible shock for them, poor souls!"

"So horrible that when Jane arrived fifteen months later, the Carews both vowed that she should never go to school."

"But," Miss Ferrars said, "if they didn't send her to school, what *did* they do?"

"Travelled with a nanny until she was six. Then they had a governess. Don't make any mistake about it. Jane had set hours for lessons and nothing was allowed to disturb those. Neither was she allowed to play around the theatre too much. I rather gather neither parent actually *wants* her to take to the stage as a career, though if she inclines that way they won't stop her."

20

"But what made them change their minds?" Miss Ferrars persisted.

"Something they hadn't foreseen, Kathy. Last Christmas, the governess became engaged to someone in the Civil Service. It was understood that the wedding would not take place for at least two years, but in March he was offered a job in Canada – a good one, meaning unexpected promotion. Naturally, he wanted to take his wife with him. So Miss Dacre left before Easter, and since then Lady Carew seems to have been racing from pillar to post trying to find someone to take her place. She couldn't in the time. The Company was booked for an extended tour of Australia and New Zealand and they were sailing last week. On almost the last day Lady Carew happened to meet Mrs Gay – Tom Gay's mother. Somehow they got on to daughters and Mrs Gay seems to have given such a glowing description of the School that the Carews decided to send their precious one-and-only to us forthwith. The Head and I have been nearly going up the walls over their cables and 'phone calls, I may tell you. However, it was decided that Lady Carew should stay behind and fly out to Melbourne where the tour begins, and so be able to attend to Jane. She really meant to park herself up here for a week or two. Then something happened to change her plans and she set off yesterday from Paris, having seen Jane on the train in charge of an acquaintance who undertook to deliver her here safely. And here the child is."

"I wonder, since they had such a prejudice against boarding schools, that they didn't leave her with some friend or relation and send her to day school," Miss Derwent commented.

"Lady Carew is an only child and both her parents are dead. *His* brother is a bachelor and his sister married a naval officer stationed at present in the West Indies. *Not* the place for a girl of Jane's age, as I think you'll agree. Most of their friends are stage folk like themselves. But as a matter of fact I think our connection with all the doctors up here turned the scale in our favour. If anything should go wrong, Jane would receive the best of medical attention."

"And Sir William wanted to get the girl out of the theatrical atmosphere," said the Head's voice at the door. "I gather he isn't at all anxious – oh, you've heard that already, have you?" as one or two of the younger mistresses began to laugh.

"It's all very well," Miss Moore said thoughtfully, "but as so far she's grown up in it, I expect she'll want it all right."

Miss Yolland began to laugh.

"What's the joke?" Miss Andrews demanded.

"Her language! She calls everyone 'darling'! She even addressed me as 'darling' when I asked her how much drawing she had done." Miss Yolland giggled again. "I was stunned. 'Oh, darling, I love it, but Miss Dacre wasn't too good at it so I'm awfully afraid you won't like my efforts too frightfully. But I'd love to be able to paint and draw if I could.' Yes; believe it or not, that's what she said. I was thankful there was no one else round to hear her!"

"Rosalind! What *did* you say?" Miss Ferrars cried.

"What *could* I say? I told her I'd see how she shaped at her first lesson and then gently hinted that it wasn't the done thing to call any mistress 'darling'. What would you have done, Kathy?"

Kathy Ferrars chuckled. "I've done it already. I was quite stunned for a moment. Then I said, "Jane, at school it's enough if you say 'Miss Ferrars'. I wouldn't use 'darling' quite so much if I were you. People mightn't understand." She took it very well. Said she'd try to remember and she hoped she hadn't appeared rude."

"Ye-e-s," Nancy Wilmot said consideringly. "I should say she's a girl who can take a telling without sulking or fretting over it. I must say *I* got a shock when she informed me that she felt so *frustrated* over algebra – just like that!"

"Then where do you propose to place her?" Miss Annersley asked with interest. "Kathy, you have her for geography and maths. Your verdict, please."

"Geography, Upper IVB. Maths, except arithmetic, which she seems to know, in Lower IVA."

"For modern languages, she could even work with Inter V," Mlle took her turn. "You would not approve, no?"

Miss Annersley groaned. "I would *not*! Nor, I'm sure, would Rosalie. It sounds as if Jane's timetable is going to be complicated enough anyhow. No, no, Jeanne! Jane may take French and German with Upper IVB, and she may begin Latin, which will keep her well occupied – that is if anyone can coach her."

Miss Derwent, who had been looking at her personal timetable, spoke. "I have two free periods when I could take her. I know Jeanne hasn't too much free time for extra coaching."

Mlle looked grateful. "She seems good at languages," she said. "It should not need more than one term of coaching. I do not think she is stupid but, tout au contraire, very quick in learning."

"Then I'll take her on, and if someone else could manage another couple of periods, that should do it," Miss Derwent agreed. "She isn't touching science at all, is she? Vida, what – "

"Not on your nelly!" Miss Armitage retorted. "So far

23

as I can find out, she doesn't even know the simplest botanical terms, let alone any chemical formulae. What's more, though she was quite polite about it, she doesn't *want* to know. Let's leave it at that, shall we?"

As a result, Jane was informed that she would be in Upper IVB for most lessons, but must join Lower IVA for algebra and geometry and, as soon as she could, for Latin, in which she would have four periods of special coaching while the rest of the form were at science.

She heard this on the Monday after Prayers, Miss Annersley having sent for her to explain it all to her. She had spent Saturday and Sunday with what was now officially her own form and was growing really friendly with most of them; notably, José Helston, Dilys Edwards and Adrienne Didier, who let her see that they were quite willing to take her into their trio and make a foursome of it. Consequently, the letter she had begun on the Sunday, rejoiced the two people to whom she meant the whole world.

"You know, darlings," she wrote, "I do feel that I am going to be really happy here – as happy as I can be anywhere when I haven't you two. I think I'm going to be in Upper IVB and I've begun to make friends with two or three of the girls already. One is José Helston, who lives at Arosa. The other two are Dilys Edwards, whose father is manager of a steelworks in Wales, and Adrienne Didier, whose father is in the French Navy. I think José's father is dead. She never talks of him, anyhow. By the way, I'm so glad you made me learn to speak French and German. There are lots of French girls in my form, some German-Swiss and one or two Germans. Then we have two days a week when we have to speak French the whole time, and two days for German, so I haven't any difficulty with ordinary lessons. It would have been *too* frustrating if I didn't know enough to manage."

She wound up with messages to those of the Company whom she knew well, but she kept her letter open until Monday when she could add a postscript to announce triumphantly that she was in the same form as her friends and between that and the glorious beauty of the mountains all round, she knew she was going to enjoy her school life tremendously.

"So after all, it's as well Miss Dacre married her Peter when she did," she wound up. "She's happy and I'm happy and I hope you two are happy, too, and make a tremendous success."

But Jane had trials to face of which, as yet, she only glimpsed the merest shadows. It remained to be seen how she would stand up to them.

CHAPTER 3

Jack out for Trouble

Jane left the study where she had been hearing which was to be her form. She was thrilled with the news. Incidentally, she had contrived to give the Head a shock. That lady had explained the intricacies of her special timetable to her, adding that she hoped that these would soon end with all the extra coaching to be provided.

"Oh, I hope so," Jane said in her eager way. "Oh, darling, it's so *frustrating* having to dash from pillar to post, so the sooner I can work at everything with Upper IVb, the better all round it will be. I quite see that."

Miss Annersley managed to repress the shock she got at being spoken to like this by a pupil and said with a laugh, "That's good, Jane! And now, as this is a French day, we had better use it all the time. You do speak French, I hear."

"But yes, Madame!" Jane slipped into the tongue readily. "German also; and some Italian."

"Ah! In that case, you should have little trouble with Latin," the Head said. "Now I hear the others coming back, so you had better join them in your form room." She glanced at the great timetable for the whole school which was pinned up beside her desk. "You have arithmetic first and then my own religious knowledge. During Break, ask someone to take you to Miss Dene in the office. She will have all your books and stationery ready for you. Until then, you must share with someone. Now run along – and good hunting!"

"Thank you, Madame." Jane rose from her chair which she set back in its place, went to the door where she executed a beautiful curtsy, having been duly warned by the others that this was de rigueur with the Head, and departed to Upper IVb where she was welcomed by at least half the form since no mistress had come to them yet.

"You are with us, then?" Adrienne exclaimed. "That is good. Jean, where should Jane sit?"

A folding desk and chair had been brought in readiness and Jean had set them in the back row. José presented her with some sheets of paper and a pencil and Adrienne produced a spare notebook and some blotting-paper. Marta Semerling, next to whom she sat, offered to share her textbooks until Jane had her own, and when Miss Ferrars arrived she found them all waiting and ready for her.

At first Jane found it hard to work with a crowd of other girls. After being alone with Miss Dacre and going at her own pace, it was disconcerting to find her efforts at concentration interrupted again and again by people who asked questions – in a number of cases having to struggle for the correct French first – and frequently wanted the explanations to be repeated. However, by dint of great effort, she did manage to work two of the sums Miss Ferrars had set as a test of how much they remembered of the previous term's work and got them right first time.

As she ticked the second one, the young mistress smiled up at Jane. "Finding things a little difficult?" she queried. "Never mind; you'll soon be used to it and then you'll find you can work faster."

It was on the tip of Jane's tongue to exclaim with her usual eager friendliness. She remembered Miss Yolland's remarks just in time, however, and merely said, "Thank you, Miss Ferrars."

"But I look like having a sticky time remembering how *not* to speak to people," she thought as she went to her seat. "I must, though. I'm not having Jack Lambert accusing me of 'slobbering' again!"

Religious knowledge was a rest after this. Miss Annersley began to revise the Gospel according to St Mark which they had done that year, and Jane found that she knew quite as much as most folk about it. During Break, José and Adrienne escorted her to Miss Dene's office and helped to take the pile of textbooks and stationery awaiting her back to the form room. There they gave her a locker, before rushing her off to the Speisesaal, as the school called the dining room, for milk and biscuits.

After Break, however, Jane had algebra, and that was with Lower IVA while the rest of Upper IVB had dictée with Mlle. She gathered up her scribbler, mathematics file and textbook, tucked pens and pencils into her blazer pocket and went across the corridor to Lower IVA which was opposite. Miss Ferrars had not yet arrived so Jane, feeling very shy and uncomfortable, stood beside the door, waiting for someone to show her where to sit. She had asked someone but the girl merely flipped up an impudent chin and went on talking to the girl next her with no further notice.

Jane had expected to find things difficult here. She had already learned that the form was ruled by The Gang and that Jack Lambert bossed The Gang. Where that select body led, almost all the others followed like young sheep. Jane tried to catch someone's eye, but the moment she looked at a girl, that person became too much engrossed in someone else to pay any heed to her. Unfortunately, Miss Ferrars was unusually late for her, having been detained by the Head for a good ten minutes. By the time she did arrive, Jane was still standing, clutching her belongings and very pink in the face.

Miss Ferrars' eyebrows shot up at the sight. "Girls!" she said sharply. "Has no one found a place for Jane Carew? What are you thinking about?"

The form had been looking as angelic as in them lay, but at this pointed question, they lost their demure air and shuffled uneasily.

"Well?" Miss Ferrars said as no one spoke. "I am still waiting for an answer. And Jane is waiting for a chair and a desk. You were told that she was joining you for algebra, were you not?" She looked straight at Barbara Hewett, the form prefect, and that young person went scarlet.

"I – er – I forgot," she stammered in French with the vilest accent.

Miss Ferrars promptly requested her to repeat her words and when at last she was satisfied with the accent, demanded another answer to her question. "You cannot have forgotten, for you were told before Break and warned to bring in an extra chair and desk. The truth, if you please, Barbara!" .

"If you please, there are not any spare desks here," Jack chipped in, seeing that Barbara was silent from confusion.

"Is your name 'Barbara'? I thought not. Barbara, I am waiting."

Barbara appeared to be unable to utter and already fifteen minutes of the lesson had gone. Miss Ferrars sent one girl for a chair and another for a desk, and when they arrived and Jane was seated at last, she swept them into such a merciless drilling in the use of brackets that they were not likely to forget it in a hurry.

Jane already had a sketchy knowledge of the rule, but with Miss Ferrars' lucid explanations, she got it fixed in her mind that morning, which was more than most of them did. They were full of resentment, partly on Jack's behalf, but a good deal on their own, and as they didn't stop to think that much of Miss Ferrars' wrath might have been saved if they had seen that a chair and desk were ready for the new girl, they laid the blame entirely on Jane. Jane felt their resentment, but she forced it to the back of her mind, gave her attention to the lesson, and when they were set to working sundry examples had the best showing of them all. Jack, who had spent her time glowering at Jane and hating her with a most unpraiseworthy vim, failed ignominiously to get a single sum right and returned to her seat with no marks and ears burning from a well-deserved rebuke. Mercifully, when the lesson ended, Jane saw no more of Lower IVA that morning.

Her next ordeal came in the afternoon when the two forms came together for an hour's games. Miss Burnett, the PT mistress, decided to test for form cricket teams and turned the others over to Monica Caird, the Games prefect, and four more of the prefects who were free during the period for tennis.

Jane confessed that she knew nothing about cricket though her father ran an eleven from the members of the Company. Tennis she had played a good deal, so she was sent to make up a four with Kitty Anderson and Jack Lambert from Lower IVB and Annette Orange from her own form.

Jack and Kitty were both certainties for their form's Eleven, and Annette wore glasses and was too nervous in consequence ever to make a good cricketer.

Monica welcomed them by sending them off to one of the tennis match courts. Margot Maynard was there in charge of all three match courts. She paired them off in an impartial manner, partnering Jack with Kitty and Jane with Annette.

"Toss for service, Jack," she said.

Jack tossed and won, which left side for Jane and Annette. When they were in place, Margot went to start off another four, leaving them with a few words of warning.

"Watch your stance, Annette. I seem to remember that foot-faulting was a trick of yours last summer. Jack – no poaching, please; and Kitty, watch your follow-through. Jane, I'll be keeping a lookout for any faults, so play your best." Then she went off and Jack prepared to serve the first ball to Jane. It was intended to beat her, but Jack had misjudged her length and it went out. The next was skied and Jane, ready for it, smashed it down as hard as she could. Kitty gaped at it and let it pass her, though it was well in.

The next service, to Annette, was better, though by no means up to Jack's usual standard. Annette returned it neatly and Kitty took it and drove to Jane, who returned it with that most maddening of returns – a slow dribble over the net. Margot had left her second four and come to attend to the first just in time to see both Kitty and Jack let it go.

"Why didn't you try to return it?" she demanded. "Yes, Jack; I know it lay practically dead, but that doesn't mean you stand there like a pillar of salt and do nothing about it. What's the score, someone?"

"Love-thirty," Kitty said.

"Then play up, you two. This won't do!"

However, the play on the part of the two younger girls showed no improvement, though Margot waxed sarcastic and gave full rein to her tongue. When the four had

31

finished their five games, all of which Jack and Kitty lost, she sent them off to the practice-board with the remark that she hoped they would try to work up their play for the rest of the period.

Kitty and Jack marched off together. Annette, who was slow, was still screwing her racquet into its press, so Margot told Jane to go after the lower form girls and not wait.

"They'll show you where to go," she added as she turned to welcome the next four. "Work at your back-hand, Jane. It's weak."

Neither of the pair in front took the slightest notice of Jane. They stalked ahead, leaving her to follow or not as she chose. It was not a pleasant position for her, but she went after them and when she reached the practice-boards saw, among the crowd of Lower IVA folk gathered round, Wilma Summers from her own form. She was thankful to see Wilma, though she barely knew her as yet. Not that she was much help. She was a sheep of a girl, running with the crowd and rarely voicing an opinion of her own. She grinned feebly at Jane, but made no effort to talk to her.

The boards were all full and Jane had to stand aside, waiting for a turn.

"Wonder she doesn't run to someone and ask them to write to her mammy and tell her about the nasty horrid girls being unkind to her baby!" Jack said loudly.

Wanda, who was there, looked worried. "Do be quieter, Jack," she murmured. "She'll hear you."

"Then she shouldn't listen!" Jack retorted. "Oh, dry up, Wanda! I'll talk as I like!"

As she was silly enough to say all this in English, it served her right that Len Maynard, coming to take her turn at coaching, reached them in time to overhear this.

Jack's first intimation that the prefect was there came when Len's voice behind her said coldly, "Have you forgotten that this is French day? Pay a fine, please. Yes, Celia?" as Celia Everett came up.

"Please, Len, we've had our half-hour here. May we go and see if we can have a court?" Celia asked, indicating her friends, Val Gardiner, Corinne Sambeau and Meg Walton.

"Very well. Jane, have you had your practice yet?"

"I've been playing on one of the courts," Jane said in her prettily-accented French.

"Well, there's a place vacant now. What's your worst point?"

"Margot told me to practise backhand strokes."

"Right! Get on with it, then. Kitty, I seem to remember you don't follow through properly. Come along and have a shot at it. Jack, take that place, and Annette," as that young woman trailed up, "here's a place for you. Get to work!"

Under Len's stern eye, Jack had to hold her tongue. She took it out in slashing at the ball in a way that called a rebuke down on her. Jane, working hard at her backhand and missing two balls out of three, received careful instruction, and Jack glowered more than ever as Len demonstrated the action in friendly manner.

The bell rang ten minutes later, so Jack had to bottle up her rage; but the result was to make her as trying during needlework as ever she had been. She fidgeted, she broke three needles, she sewed with stitches of such size and irregularity that Mlle told her to unpick them and start all over again. That was where she topped up her iniquities by muttering angrily that she hated sewing, anyhow, and would never be able to do it and she didn't care, *anyhow;* adding to her sins by speaking in English. Mlle was a patient person, but this was too much for her.

"Report yourself to your form mistress for impertinence, Jacynth," she said sharply, using Jack's proper name to emphasize her annoyance. "This evening after Prayers you may come to me and I will instruct you in the art of hemming."

Jack had a rude reply on the tip of her tongue, but Wanda, who was sitting beside her, gave her a secret nudge. Since Jack was not altogether lost to reason, she took the hint and Mlle, ignoring her glare, went on to the next girl.

All the same, Jack had to express her fury some way and she did it in a manner that filled her with shame whenever she thought of it later. At the end of the lesson, she stuck out a foot just as Jane passed her to put away her work and workbox in the cupboard. Away went Jane and away went the workbox, scattering its contents far and wide and ending up with a crash against the side of the great porcelain stove. Jane was merely shaken, but when someone picked up the box, the lid hung loosely from one hinge and the slips of wood dividing the top tray into compartments had all come out.

No one had seen Jack's action but Jane, who had been too late to save herself. She scorned to tell tales, only explaining in answer to Mlle's questions that she had tripped and no, she wasn't hurt, thank you.

Mlle expressed her regret at the damage to the workbox, which was new. Some of Jane's own form helped to gather up the needles and cottons and other oddments. Mlle took the box to ask Gaudenz, the man-of-all-work, to mend it and there, to all appearances, the episode ended. But Jane was bewilderedly asking herself *why* Jack Lambert should treat her like this; and Jack, the worst of her present ill-humour relieved, found to her dismay that she was feeling a complete cad. It made things worse that she couldn't tell Jane she was sorry, or even make a formal apology. She contented herself with behaving for the rest of the day like a bear with a sore paw so that finally even her most faithful followers sheered off when she came near. And that was another thing for which she most unfairly blamed Jane. But Jack was in the mood to be thoroughly unfair just then. It would be some time before she could feel anything else where Jane Carew was concerned.

CHAPTER 4

Jack Excels Herself

By the end of a fortnight Jane had more or less settled down at school. She and José Helston were well on the way to becoming chums. In form, she was finding her feet with surprising ease, once she had learned to shut out sundry distractions. She had joined the School clubs open to people over thirteen and she was learning to live with other girls and make allowances for any difference between their points of view and her own – a big step forward for a girl brought up as she had been. Her worst trouble was still Jack Lambert.

Jack remained implacable where Jane was concerned, with the result that Jack, never an easy character, grew more and more difficult and was forever in trouble. Her cheeky little face wore an almost continuous scowl. She was so touchy that a number of her friends sheered off from her. Her work deteriorated to a degree that earned her an unpleasant interview with the Head. In short, she was a problem all round.

"*I* don't know what's wrong with Jack Lambert!" Miss Bertram suddenly snapped one evening when she had spent twenty minutes scoring out line after line of something Jack was pleased to call a composition. "She seems to be taking leave of her senses!"

"I'd like to wring her neck!" Miss Andrews chipped in. "Just look at this dictation! Her spelling's never been her strong point; but for a girl of nearly fourteen to make

36

such idiotic mistakes in words like 'hospital' and 'doctor' is beyond the limit!''

"How *has* she spelt them?" Kathy Ferrars demanded, craning her neck to see. The next moment she broke into peals of laughter.

"What's the joke?" Miss Derwent asked plaintively.

"Jack! Sharlie, what *can* possess her?"

"Your guess is as good as mine! And look how she's divided 'legend'!''

Everyone near stretched to see. Jack had made it into "leg-end" and the staff room rang with their mirth.

"What about the other words?" Miss Derwent demanded when she had recovered. "How *has* she spelt them – though I'd believe anything of her after 'leg-end'," she added, her voice wobbling ominously.

Very solemnly, Sharlie Andrews spelt out, " 'Hospertell' and 'dockter', and that's not much worse than more than half the other words. Honestly!''

"This is mad," Miss Derwent said decidedly. "Jack can spell well enough when she likes. What's gone wrong with the child?''

No one could tell her. No one had ever expected tomboy Jack to resent so fiercely being moved to another dormitory, even though they all knew that she regarded Len Maynard as her special mentor.

"Her age, I suppose," Nancy Wilmot said thoughtfully. "The early teens are a tricky time. You're neither a child nor grown-up and you don't know what to make of yourself. I remember what *I* was like at that age. All the same, it's no excuse for that sort of work.''

Kathy Ferrars considered. "That may be something to do with it, Nance, but it's more than that. Something has upset Jack pretty badly.''

"Well what, then?" Sharlie Andrews inquired.

"Goodness knows! But I'm going to find out. This sort of thing can't be allowed to go on."

"I doubt if you or any of us will do much with her," Miss Derwent said sceptically. "Better turn Len Maynard on to her."

They left it at that. Time never stood still and there were piles of file-papers to be looked over and marked. Jack and her problems must wait at present.

The prefects were as puzzled as the staff over Jack's general attitude. She slouched about, snapped and snarled at all and sundry, and more than once came within an ace of being reported for impertinence.

Aimée Robinet, usually the most amiable of beings, arrived in the prefects' room one afternoon with set lips and angry eyes. Only Lizette Falence, the music prefect, and Len Maynard were there. The rest all had games; but Lizette had had an unexpected violin lesson and Len had turned an ankle during the morning walk and was under orders to keep her foot up as much as possible for the next day or two. Lizette was using the time to work out the fingering of a new study and was absorbed. Len, who had been giving only languid attention to *The Taming of the Shrew*, glanced up as her compeer stalked in. What she saw in Aimée's face made her drop her book.

"Aimée, qu'as-tu?" she demanded.

Aimée tossed down the racquet and net of balls she was carrying. "I am enraged!" she announced – quite needlessly.

"You look like it. Who or what has enraged you?" Len queried. "*You* aren't given to losing your temper."

"It is Jack – Jack Lambert, Len. We all know that Jack will hear you. Can you not speak to her about her rudeness? Indeed, she has been really impudent to me."

"*What?*" Len's eyebrows shot up into her curly chestnut

hair. "You sit down and tell me exactly what she's done. Lizette, give that music a rest and listen to this."

Lizette raised dreamy eyes from her work. "Give me but one little moment more, Len. I cannot see how to finger this phrase – ah! I have him! So – and *so* – and *so*!" She lifted her fiddle to her shoulder and played it over soundlessly. "At last! And now I can work at it properly." She laid down her fiddle and bow and turned to Len. "And now, Len, what is it you would say?"

"Not me – Aimée," Len said. "Oh, stop messing about with that music, Lizette! Here!" She leaned forward and twitched the book of studies from under Lizette's hand. "I'm sitting on this for the moment. Go ahead, Aimée!"

"It is Jack," Aimée began; and at that name, Lizette groaned.

"Jack Lambert is a – she is very, very trying, Len. Do you not find her so?"

"I haven't seen much of her since we came back," Len confessed. "For one thing she's in another dormy now. And then whenever I could I've been along to San to visit Aunt Grizel. I couldn't leave her – not after the way she saved my life during the hols.[1] Anyhow, I'm awfully fond of her. But go on, Aimée, I can't speak to Jack unless I know rather more about the business than I do at the moment."

Aimée and Lizette both glanced at her sympathetically. They knew from just what danger "Aunt Grizel' had saved her. Indeed, when the school at large heard the story it had been instantly suggested that though Grizel Cochrane was an Old Girl and no longer a pupil, she should be awarded the school's own medal for courage.

Aimée had calmed down a little now and she continued

[1] *Chalet School Reunion.*

more quietly, "Our tennis set had just finished and we were resting in the pavilion–"

"Who, exactly?" Len asked.

"Ted Grantley, your sister Con, Suzanne Kiefen and me."

"No one else – within earshot, I mean?"

"But no. All the others were either playing or resting elsewhere. Does it matter?"

"I don't know – it might. Go on, Aimée. Sorry I interrupted."

"Ça ne fait rien!" Aimée cast a fleeting smile at Len before she continued. "We were talking together when Jack came to us. She had brought a message for Suzanne. Len, I do not know if you have observed how badly Jack is deporting herself this term? You have seen – no?"

"Do you mean behaviour?" Lizette asked.

Aimée made a gesture. "Oh, for that, her behaviour is always bad this term. But I meant the way she bears herself. She stoops and she–" she paused to hunt for the English word.

"She slouches," Len said. "Yes; I've noticed and I meant to say something to her about it. I'll attend to it this very day."

Aimée went on with her story. "I called to her to come to me and said she must straighten her back or she would become bossue and I was she would not like it. I did not speak in an angry voice, Len, but she regarded me d'un air farouche. Then she said, 'Let me alone! I'm sick of being picked on!' And what does that mean, my Len?"

"Oh – tracasser – gronder contre – either will do," Len said quickly. "Did she really say that to you, Aimée?"

"But yes; and more. I asked if she felt ill and she said she did not, but she was fed up with people always going

40

for her – and I know what *that* means – and I – well," Aimée became very pink, "I could just shut my head."

Len sat up with a bang. "She said that to a prefect? She must have gone bats! What did you do – send her to report herself? She jolly well deserves it! Don't say you passed it over."

"But no; I told her to report herself for rudeness and – and she said, 'You've got a hope!' Then she ran away and I was so angry, I left the others for I did not wish to lose my temper. But Len, do you think she is, perhaps, ill? For in that case, I should speak to Matey, n'est-ce-pas?"

"Ill my foot!" Len retorted inelegantly. "That's plain temper and nothing else. OK, Aimée! Leave it to me! I'll have a word or two with Miss Jack and she'll be coming to you with her tail between her legs to apologize humbly before she goes off to make that report! I promise you *that*!"

Aimée looked doubtful. To her mind Jack, in her present state, was unlikely to take a scolding from even Len without a murmur.

Lizette shook her head. "I do not think it will do, Len. Why Jack has been so much trouble all this term, I do not know; but it is all the same thing."

"Is there, perhaps, trouble at her home?" Aimée suggested.

"If it was that, it would affect young Anne as well," Len said shrewdly. "I was talking to Anne at Mittagessen and she was just as usual. She's not much like Jack's sister, is she?" she added. "She's a nice kid, but she's – well – *colourless*."

"Rather let us say that Jack is all alive and always makes a stir," Lizette suggested. She turned to Aimée.

"Surely, Aimée, you do not think she will refuse to report herself when she has been commanded to do so?"

"I do not know. In her present mood, I think she might."

"I hope not, for her own sake," Len said ominously. "That crowd doesn't do that sort of thing as a rule, though. Look here, Aimée, let it ride for the moment, will you. Jack might cheek you if she was in a rage – though that doesn't excuse her abominable rudeness – but I doubt if she'd disobey a direct order like that. After all, she may play the ass, but she *has* got sense enough."

In the end they left it like that. In any case, the bell rang and the others came in and they all had to collect their books and go down to the library for a lecture from the Head on "The Eighteenth-century Essayist". Miss Annersley was a fascinating lecturer and, in the interest of what she said, Jack and her doings passed out of their heads for the time being.

Kaffee und Kuchen, the Chalet School substitute for tea in Switzerland, followed, and Len was on one of the urns which meant that, when she had filled her quota of cups, she went to the prefects' table herself. After that, there was just time to change for the evening and then she had to go off to take prep duty with Upper III.

Len's lameness slowed her down a little, so she took a short cut through a corridor the girls were not supposed to use, though prefects might. As she limped along, she heard voices from the far end – voices she recognized. She quickened her pace slightly, turned a corner sharply, and came on an unpleasant little scene. The new girl, Jane Carew, was standing with her back to the wall. She was paler than usual, though her head was well up and her grey eyes looked almost black. Facing her was Jack Lambert, as red as Jane was white and with a nasty little smile on her lips. Both girls were so absorbed in their own encounter that they never heard the prefect's halting step until she was almost on them, and Len heard enough to assure her that Jack was baiting Jane.

"Did the poor little baby run to its mammy with all sorts of tales about the nasty girls?" Jack jeered while Jane, unaccustomed to this sort of thing, stared at her in silence. "Did it want a nice nanny to look after it and tuck it up in bed at nights and kiss it when–"

She got no further. At this point a firm hand gripped one shoulder and she looked up straight into Len's face. The smile vanished, giving place to a look of consternation at what she saw in the violet-grey eyes that held hers whether she would or not. Jack might be impudent to other prefects, but Len was a different matter. From the very first she had admired and liked the prefect. A real friendship existed between them. But Jack could see no friendliness in the stern gaze Len had fixed on her and inwardly she cringed.

There was silence for a full minute. Then Len spoke and her words were icy. "That will do, Jacynth. Go to your form room at once. I will see you about this later. Go, I say!"

Jack had managed to look away while Len was speaking. Now she glanced at her again, and under the look she got she wilted completely. The furious colour left her cheeks, her long lashes dropped and, obeying the prefect's command, she turned and literally *crawled* away. Len then dealt with Jane.

"I don't know if you know, Jane, but no one but staff and prefects may use this corridor, and certainly not during school-hours."

Jane pulled herself together. She had seen Jack coming and had slipped into the corridor to avoid meeting her.

Jack had made it plain that, for her own reasons, she hated the new girl. They never encountered each other without Jack bestowing a baleful glare on her. If they happened to be alone, she always had something hurtful to say and Jane, sensitive and too proud to reply in the same manner, had only silence for her armour. Silence was not much help in such circumstances and Jane was beginning to steer clear of the enemy on every possible occasion.

"Yes, I did know," she said now in answer to Len's query. "I forgot. I'm so sorry."

The iciness vanished as the elder girl smiled down into the grey eyes raised to hers. "Well, don't forget again," she said. "It really is a rule, and you people have plenty of other ways of getting round the place without prancing along here. Understand?"

The colour had come back into Jane's face under this treatment. "I do and I really will try to remember," she promised.

"Good! Now you'll have to scram or you'll be late for prep. You've exactly two minutes to get there."

"Oh, darling, I must fly!" Jane exclaimed, herself again. "We have Francie Wilford on duty tonight and you can't imagine what a dirty look she can give you if you aren't punctual! I will remember, though – and thanks a million!"

Len was stupefied into utter silence. She watched Jane scuttering back along the corridor until she was out of sight. Then, as the light footsteps died away, she pulled herself together and went on to her destination, a broad grin lighting up her face.

"Gosh! What *have* we collected this time?" she asked herself as she limped into IIIA, her lips straight again, though her eyes were still dancing with amusement. "I

44

think I'd better cultivate Jane Carew a little. She'll be quite a novel experience for me! Besides it'll be something new to tell Aunt Grizel when I visit her on Saturday. Won't she yell, though!"

CHAPTER 5

A Straight Talk with Jack

It was next day before Len was able to get hold of Jack for the promised talk. That young woman had come to her senses sufficiently to obey Aimée's behest and go to report herself for rudeness. As this had happened before, Miss Bertram, her form mistress, gave her a severe talking-to and, after sending for the prefect so that Jack might apologize in proper form, condemned the sinner to early bed that night.

"Perhaps a little extra time to think will help you to realize that insolence to prefects is insolence to the Head," she said scathingly. "You know quite well that among you girls they are her representatives. May I ask if you would have spoken to Miss Annersley in the same way?"

As she knew very well that she would never have dared, Jack hung her head in silence. Miss Bertram said no more, but she saw to it that the culprit marched off to bed as soon as Prayers were over, where Matey, happening to meet her on the way to her dormitory, instantly demanded to know what she was doing, got the story from her, and added her own strictures. Jack accepted them meekly enough. No girl had yet been found to be hardy enough to outface Matey for long. Nevertheless, when she was finally sent off with tingling ears, she was seething inwardly. All she realized in the time that elapsed before she went to sleep was that she was at odds with most of the world and it was all because of that wretched Jane Carew.

Meanwhile, Len had contrived to give a fair amount of serious thought to how she was to deal with Jack. It was as well for that young person that Len possessed the gift of understanding to a high degree – a gift she had inherited from her mother. As the eldest of a long family of eleven, Len had known responsibility from an early age and, where a good many girls of sixteen would have contented themselves with a lecture and left it at that, she considered seriously how best she could get through the shell of ill-feeling and naughtiness with which Jack had concealed her normal side. It would be no easy task, but Len had had much the same thing to do with the youngest of her triplet sisters, though she didn't think that Margot's troubles in the least resembled Jack's.

It was between the end of the Junior Middles' prep and Abendessen that she found her opportunity. Glancing out of the library window where she was looking up some notes on the German poets, she saw a bunch from Lower IIIB making for the playing-fields. Some way behind them came Jack, alone for a wonder. Len dropped her pen, ran to the open window and called.

"Jack – Jack Lambert! Attends, s'il te plaît! Je voudrais parler à toi!"

Jack stopped short and came up to the window laggingly. "Vous désirez?" she asked with a growl.

Len gave her an amused glance. "Attends-moi! Je viens!" She snatched up her belongings, thrust them into an empty filing-drawer and hurried out. There was a risk that if she kept Jack waiting, that young person might go off and this was too good a chance to miss. She sped round the corner of the house, still limping slightly. She paid no heed to her discomfort, but reached the spot where Jack was standing, hunched up in a most unpromising attitude.

"I want to talk to you," she said, dropping into English. "Yes," as Jack gave her a surprized look, "I know this is French day, but it's all right. I give you permission to speak in English and I'm using English myself. Come along!"

With a hand on the slim shoulder, she steered Jack away from the house and along a small arbour where she pushed her down on a rustic seat, took the only other herself, and leaned her chin on her clasped hands.

"Jack," she said, "why are you sitting in a heap like that? Is your back aching?"

"I'm all right," Jack growled, nevertheless straightening he shoulders.

"That's better! For goodness sake, stop going round as if you were old Atlas himself with the whole weight of the world on top of you!"

Jack said nothing, but she looked less sulky. Len contemplated her. She was paler than usual and there were shadows under her eyes. They were into May now and the day had been hot. The prefect fished in a pocket and produced a stick of cologne ice.

"Rub your face and hands with that," she said, pushing it across the rustic table at which they were seated. "It'll cool you a little."

Jack stared, but she obeyed without comment. When she handed the stick back, she felt soothed somehow. She certainly was cooler. This place was well away from everyone and was very quiet. Finally, Len's friendly manner helped. She had almost thought last night that their friendship was at an end for ever. Suddenly she heaved a deep sigh.

"What's the way of that?" Len asked, using the ice

herself, and still speaking in English. She had decided on this, for languages were not Jack's strong point and she felt that, in her present state, the younger girl would be quite unable to express herself with any freedom in another language. She added, "You may speak English as I told you."

"Thank goodness!" Jack said with another sigh. Then she fell silent.

Len left her to herself for a minute or two. Then she spoke again, choosing her words with care. "What's wrong, Jack? You aren't like yourself at all. Quite well, aren't you?"

"I'm OK," Jack said gruffly.

"No trouble at home, I hope?"

"Not so far as I know." Jack was completely laconic.

"Then what's wrong? Tell me, Jack." Her voice was very persuasive.

"Oh, I don't know," Jack said. She paused; then it came with a rush. "I – I'm all no-how! I – I – things are all such a *muddle!*"

Len sent a swift silent prayer up for help and wisdom. Then she said gently, "It's Jane Carew, isn't it? Why don't you like her, Jack? She seems quite a decent sort to me, though I haven't seen a lot of her, even if she is in my dormy."

"*Like* her?" Jack drew a long breath. Then it tumbled out. "I *loathe* her – *loathe* and *hate* and *despise* and *detest* her!"

She waited then, wondering if Len would hurl her forth or treat her to a sermon on the wickedness of such feelings. Len did neither.

"Oh?" she said in a calmly interested voice. "Why?"

Jack shuffled her feet. "Oh – I don't know," she muttered.

"Why not? That's not reasonable. Has she been unpleasant to you?"

As all the unpleasantness had been on Jack's side, this was a nasty question and Jack made no effort to answer it.

"I think," Len said slowly, "I'd better tell you something about Jane's history – why she's not like most of the run of our girls. It may help you to understand her better and that's always something."

"I'm not interested," Jack growled.

"No? All the same – " Len paused before she added, "What I'm going to say is in confidence, Jack. Don't tell anyone else, please."

"OK!" It came with a growl.

"I got it from my mother last Sunday. For some reason, it's being kept quiet at the moment, but I can trust you. Jane's father is the big actor-manager, Sir William Carew."

This meant nothing to Jack who was no reader and whose visits to the theatre had been mainly to see the Christmas pantomime in the big city near her home.

"What's that got to do with it?" she demanded.

"Everything! Listen!" And Len began to tell the story of Jane's early life which her mother had told her. Jack listened, at first because she must; presently, from sheer interest.

Halfway through, she interrupted Len to ask, "Has she *really* been all over the world like that?"

Len nodded. "She has."

"But – but – why didn't they send her to school?"

Len had not been very sure how much to tell her junior. Now she decided to give her the whole story as she had heard it. She went on and as she listened, the last of

Jack's sullenness vanished and she looked like her old self.

"So you see," the prefect wound up, "Jane's oddities are the result of her earlier life. She's been with people who sometimes gush, so she gushes on occasions; just as," she added with a grin, "you sometimes come out with bits of Cheshire dialect that you've been hearing all your life."

Jack turned a bright puce. Then she remembered her grievance. "It wasn't just that," she mumbled, "though I do think she says the maddest things."

"I know. You were furious at being sent to another dormy for the sake of a new girl."

"Well, I *didn't* like being chucked out like that – leaving all my pals!"

"But my dear girl, it happens to all of us sooner or later!" Len exclaimed. "How many dormies do you think *I've* been in? *Five*, no less! You've been jolly lucky that it hasn't happened before."

Jack's eyes widened. "Gosh! I never thought of that. I – well, I thought I'd be stuck in Pansy till I was a Senior Middle, anyhow."

"Not very likely!" Len spoke with authority.

Jack was silent. Then she brought out the core of the matter. "The thing is that I never get a chance to see you when I want to know something. Pris Dawbarn is all right, but she doesn't know things – not like you."

With a swift memory of some of Jack's questions, Len agreed. She had been hard put to it herself to answer some of the younger girl's queries. Priscilla was a pleasant girl and a good worker, but otherwise, she seemed content to skim on the surface of things and Jack had a trick of sometimes going deep.

"I'm sorry about that," she said seriously. "I'm very

busy, of course. This is always a full term and with an important exam on top of everything else, I haven't had much time to spare. When I have, I've been off to the San to Aunt Grizel. You know how she rescued me during the house-party Mother gave for some of the Old Girls during the hols. She's damaged her back and it's going to mean weeks of lying in plaster, so of course I do all I can to cheer her up. But I didn't mean to neglect you. Any time you've something really important to ask, latch on to me and I'll do my best for you. But it must be really important," she added warningly. "Things that aren't you can find out for yourself if you must. What do you think the library's for?"

"Yes; but often things I want to know aren't library things."

"No; but you're old enough to try to work out the smaller ones for yourself. We all have to do it sooner or later."

"I see. I'll try not to worry you too much, then."

Jack was silent and Len glanced at her anxiously. She knew that although she had brought the younger girl to a more reasonable frame of mind, they had only touched on the fringes of the trouble. Jack must find a new outlook and Len was uncertain what more to say to help her to it. Wisely, she decided to leave it for the present. Telling Jack some of Jane's history was unlikely to achieve much just yet. What Jack needed was a new attitude to Jane. She glanced at her watch and gave an exclamation.

"Only five minutes left! Anything more to say, Jack?"

"Why did Matey pick on me and not one of the others?"

"I imagine because she thought you were sensible enough not to make a fuss about it. In any case, it had nothing to do with Jane, so why bully her?"

"Bullying!" Jack went scarlet. "I – I – "

"Of course you did! Judging by what I overheard last night, you've been utterly beastly to her. And that, let me tell you, is something I never expected from you, of all people. It gave me a nasty shock, I can tell you!"

"I – I didn't mean it that way."

"Jack, you aren't a baby now. You're fourteen in three months' time and that's not a baby – or shouldn't be. It was extra unpleasant because things can't be too easy for Jane. She's been uprooted completely and tossed headlong into an entirely new kind of life. I should say she had more than enough on her plate without you treating her like that. What's more, I'll bet your gang have followed suit. You lead that lot by the nose and you know it!"

Jack had nothing to say. She sat there feeling, to quote herself, utterly wormish. Len rubbed it in.

"You see, Jack, you've a lot of responsibility where that crew are concerned. They think you're the cat's pyjamas. What you do, they'll do. If you're decent, they'll be decent. If you're the other thing, so will they be. You're a born leader. It's something you can't help and so long as you try to lead well, it's a good thing."

"Well, I just wish they wouldn't," Jack growled.

"Funking it?" Len asked gravely. "That won't help. Listen, Jack. Before so many years are up, you and your crowd will be prefects. What prefects are, to a very large extent the School is. Now, are you going on as you've been this term, becoming a bully and an unpleasant creature? Setting the Juniors an example of that kind? Or are you going to pull up, be the pleasant girl you've always been until this, and help to keep the School what we've all tried to make it? For that's what it boils down to. There goes the bell for the end of prep, so we must go

53

now. But you think it over. And Jack – I don't like preaching, but if it's hard, you haven't far to go to seek for help. See what I mean?" Len got the last words out with an effort. In some ways, she was extremely reserved and it was a struggle for her to speak of deeper things, especially to a girl so much younger.

Jack darted a quick glance at her. "OK," she said gruffly. "I know. And – and – I'll let young Jane alone after this. I must scram!"

She fled from the arbour, leaving Len to follow in rather more dignified style, hoping as she went that what she had said would bear fruit. In some ways, Jack was a very unknown quantity.

"But at least she's promised to let Jane alone, so I've accomplished so much," the girl thought as she moved slowly to the house. "For the rest only time will show."

CHAPTER 6

VA Want Jane

Jack did think over what Len had said to her. More than once she cringed inwardly as she remembered that accusation of bullying. She was, as Len had told her, a decent girl at bottom. It came as a shock to realize how far she had fallen beneath her own standards.

"No one's going to have another chance to call me a bully," she thought. "And I s'pose I'll have to do what I can to keep the rest off Jane's bones. Oh, bother Len! – bother her – *bother* her! Why did she have to say that? I don't want it and I don't see why I should have to have it. Why can't the others take their own line? They've got minds, same as I have. Surely they're not *forced* to follow me?"

This was the same night, when she lay going hot and cold by turns as she remembered Len's trenchant words. It was almost a relief to think of Jane for a change.

"I don't think I can ever like her," she thought. "I've loathed her too much for that. Oh, I do wish she'd never come to make me nasty!"

She fell asleep at last, still resenting the present state of affairs. She woke up resenting it, but at least Len had gone some way to reconciling her to accepting it. In between paying a certain amount of attention to her lessons that day, she went on trying to worry things out for herself. Finally, by the Saturday, she had made up her mind. In Break, she summoned the Gang, marched

55

them off to a private spot and informed them firmly that, for the future, they were to lay off Jane Carew.

They heard her with some amazement. During the last few days she seemed to have come back to herself and they were only too glad to accept her leadership once more. As Gillie Garstin had said, Jack did get things done.

"Do you mean we are to be friendly with her?" Wanda von Eschenau gasped.

"Friendly – but no need to be pally," Jack said coolly. "Leave her alone and – and be polite. That's all." She turned to Gillie. "Come on, Gill! They're making a lily-pond down in the rock-garden. Let's go and see what they're doing."

Gillie went off with her and, once they were gone, the others closed ranks and discussed the latest thoroughly. Just what had brought about the change, no one was prepared to say; but Len had been quite right when she said Jack led them by the nose. They might question her decisions, but on the whole they would always follow where she led.

As a result, during the next few days Jane found that, while they were hardly to be described as forthcoming, they were polite enough. She was as startled as anyone at first. Then she decided that whatever it was that had made them dislike her must have vanished and she became her usual eager, friendly self when she was with them. They met her overtures with reserve, but at least they did not snub her and no one was actively unkind.

As for Jack, though rather more subdued than usual, she had lost the black dog which had lived on her shoulders ever since term began. Her work improved once more so that the staff were able to relax where she was concerned, and the prefects ceased to look out for trouble with her.

Jane herself found that with the teaching she was getting, both in form and privately, she was making strides. She was a clever girl and had been taught to work hard. Having determined not to stay a day longer than she must with a lower form for anything, she worked even harder than usual. Latin she found comparatively easy, with her knowledge of other languages and her genuine gift for them. Mlle de Lachennais testing her at the end of the first month was amazed to find how far she had gone.

Miss Derwent laughed. "Jane laps up Latin as a cat laps cream," she said.

"But, Ruth chérie, what a simile!" Mlle exclaimed, laughing.

"Awfully apt, though!" Kathy Ferrars joined in their talk. "It describes her exactly. She's got brains, that kid."

After that, the talk drifted off onto other paths.

The fourth Thursday of term arrived and with it, a problem for the members of VA.

It was the custom for the upper forms to take it in turns to entertain the school on Saturday evenings. Sometimes they had dancing and games; sometimes the form concerned gave a show of some kind; sometimes, though this happened mostly during the Christmas and spring terms, they ran competitions with little prizes.

Being an ambitious form, VA had chosen to give a play which had been written by two of their members – Eloïse Dafflon, a Swiss girl, and Priscilla Dawbarn, who had a gift for scribbling verse that the austere Miss Derwent called doggerel for the most part. Incidental music had been composed by Zita Roselli, whose great passion was her violin. The story was dramatic, and one of the principal characters had to be a little girl. The part had been unanimously awarded to Tina Harms, a tiny creature with a mass of flaxen hair who, despite her fairylike appearance, was the form's best mathematician and intended to take up accountancy when her schooldays ended.

The gifted authors, who were, nominally at least, also joint producers, had had a hard time of it drilling Tina, who had the looks but was no actress. Still, at the last rehearsal she had given a fairly adequate performance, so their dismay can be judged when, on the Thursday, Tina went down with a severe bilious attack.

"What *are* we to do now?" Ruey Richardson demanded of the form after Matron had left them with the information that Tina would certainly not be able to play on Saturday – and probably not be well enough even to watch.

"Is there *no* one else?" Mary Allen, the form prefect asked frantically.

"Who, for instance? 'Aubert' has to carry her in and hold her in his arms for at least seven minutes. If you can see Gerda carrying any of *us* for more than two seconds, I can't! And that's flat!" Ruey retorted.

They looked round and groaned. Gerda Nordheim, the "Aubert", had been chosen mainly on account of her size and strength. She stood five foot ten inches tall and was broad in proportion, making a sharp contrast with Tina's four foot eleven inches. Even the shortest of the others was a bare four inches less than Gerda.

"Could we ask for someone from the juniors?" Odette Mercier proposed.

"My good girl, which of the kids could learn the part in the time?" Ruey asked crossly. She was stage manager and had also helped considerably with the production. After all their hard work, Tina's illness came as a calamity. "This is Thursday and the show's on Saturday.

We go down to the lake this afternoon which means that we shan't get back much before 17.00 hours. By the time we've tidied and had Abendessen and Prayers it'll be bedtime for the kids; so that knocks out today for any work. Besides, unless we snaffle someone from the Junior Middles, we won't be much better off. The Senior Middles are a frightfully leggy lot this year."

"In any case," Eloïse pointed out, "we must have an *actress* – "

"What price Tina?" Priscilla grinned.

"But with her we have had time to teach her. And what is more, we must have a blonde with long hair, for part of the plot turns on her hair. Who is there who can be all that?" Odette cried.

"What about Wanda von Eschenau?" Marie Huber suggested.

"She'd *look* the part all right," Priscilla agreed, "but have you ever taken prep for that lot? It takes Wanda all her time to learn eight lines of ordinary poetry. She'd never manage, 'Germaine'!"

"Arda Peik – much too fat; Renata van Buren – always giggles at the wrong time; Margaret Twiss – another giggler!" Ruey sounded worried.

"What about someone from Upper IVB?" Thérèse Rambeau suggested.

"Precious little choice there. That's where the legginess begins," Priscilla pointed out. "José Helson's a good little actress, but she's as dark as they come. Elsa Behrens stammers if she gets excited and Dilys Edwards loses her head. Who else is there in that form?"

They racked their brains. Ruey gave a sudden exclamation. "I've got it – that new child, Jane Carew! She's fair enough; she's on the small side; and if heredity goes for anything, she ought to be a born actress."

"A born actress? Mais comment?" Thérèse demanded.

"Don't you know? Her dad is Sir William Carew, who goes round the world with his company acting Shakespeare and Sheridan and people like that. Aunt Joey told me," explained Ruey, who was ward and adopted daughter of Dr and Mrs Maynard.

"I believe, my Ruey, you have hit on a plan," Eloïse said slowly. "She has only come this term, so she will not have to trouble about prizes. Even, when we explain to the Head, she may consent to let her off some of her prep."

"She *may*," was all Ruey would allow herself to say.

"Of course she will!" Mary took charge. "We have only to explain and she won't say 'no' when it's so important to the play."

"Sure she won't," Priscilla said authoritatively. "And we really are in a hole, thanks to Tina's collywobbles."

"But what is that?" Gabriella Meynolles inquired.

"What is what?"

"Colly – I forget him."

Priscilla giggled. "Collywobbles? Just tummy pains, my dear. Well, folks, what about it? Do we see what the Head says? We'd better know as soon as possible. Heredity or not, it'll take Jane all her time to learn the part and get all her actions and so on. By the way, Germaine comes on singing in one scene, you remember? Has Jane a voice?"

No one knew, but as no one could think of a better substitute for Tina, they had to take it on trust. Ruey, Eloïse and Priscilla were deputed to tackle the Head as soon as possible and the two people who were mainly responsible for the dresses were ordered to be ready to do any alterations necessary to Germaine's clothes. Thérèse began to turn out Tina's possessions in search of the typed part and by the time the deputation returned from the study to report that Miss Annersley had agreed to everything they proposed and had even said, without being asked, that Jane might be excused all preparation that day and Friday, everything was ready.

There was no chance of getting hold of Jane until the afternoon. This was one of the days on which the school went down to Lake Thun for aquatic sports, so morning school ended at noon. They went down to Interlaken in the little rack-and-pinion train which went up the mountain slope, calling at various shelves where tiny platforms with roofs over them constituted the stations. The train consisted of three little coaches and as one climbed slowly upwards, its mate came sliding slowly downwards. On the first trip down to the lake, Jack and Co had watched Jane for any signs of fear. It was not unknown for new girls to dislike the train, and more than one had asked nervously what would happen if the electricity were cut off or the wires to which the great overhead trolleys were attached broke. Jane, however, took it very coolly. She had encountered this mode of travel in many other places and never turned a hair. Her only question had been how long it would take them to reach Interlaken.

The girls went down in batches, Seniors first; then Senior Middles – Junior Middles – Juniors – Kindergarten. They had their own bathing beaches which, on these special days, were roped off to the general public.

"How are we to give her the part?" Priscilla asked the others.

"Have to wait till we're all down at Thun," Ruey said.

"I wished her to have it sooner if possible," Eloïse said anxiously. "She might at least read it through during the journey. Then she could tell us at once if she thinks she can learn it in the time."

"Well, we can't do anything about it now. There's the

gong." Ruey returned. "Try during rest period if you like."

They did like. Eloïse made it her business to set up her chair by Jane's out in the grounds, and Priscilla joined them, followed by Mary. Jane was startled when the three Seniors parked themselves round her, but welcomed them with a smile.

Eloïse, having got permission to break the silence rule of rest period, pitched straight in. "Jane, you can act, n'est-ce-pas?" she asked eagerly. "I mean could you possibly take a part and do it on Saturday evening?"

"I – I might," Jane gasped, staring wide-eyed. "If it's not too long, I think I could."

"Good!" Mary took charge. "I'll explain. You know we're giving a play to you folk on Saturday night?"

Jane nodded.

"Well, Tina Harms was playing the most important part and now she's in San with a bilious attack and won't be able to do it. Could you?"

Jane had collected herself by this time. "If I might first see it," she said, holding out her hand.

They put the typescript into it and she skimmed the sheets quickly. Presently she looked up. "I think I can learn this in the time. But how about rehearsals? When can we have any?"

"This evening after Abendessen and tomorrow at the same time and Saturday morning. The Head says it's O.K. Will you do it?"

Jane flushed. "Do you really want me?"

"Shouldn't ask if we didn't," Priscilla said bluntly. "So far as looks go, you're It! If you can learn the words and act it, we'll be grateful. If not, we'll have to call the whole thing off for the present."

"If you really think I'll do, I'll do my best," Jane said.

"Then *that's* settled, thank heaven!" Mary said thankfully. "Right! You keep those, Jane, and when the others are doing prep, the Head said you could learn it instead. By the way, she's excusing all your prep till Monday for this. Thanks a lot! We didn't want to have to cancel it, but we couldn't do anything else if you couldn't come to the rescue."

"Oh, but my poppet, I'm only too pleased!" Jane cried. "Luckily, I'm a quick study. I think I can manage it by tomorrow at latest. If I have to, I must just wing through it tonight. But I can promise to know it by tomorrow."

"If you do that, we'll bless you forever!" Priscilla said fervently. "Now we'll leave you to finish the rest period. Come on, folks! Let's break the good news to the rest." She jumped up and went off, dragging her chair behind her and followed by the other two after they had added their thanks. But when they were well out of earshot, Eloïse looked at Mary.

"I can speak English as you know, Mary, but what did she mean when she said she would wing through it?"

"Not a clue! Theatre slang, I suppose, but as to what she means, you know as much as I do."

"And that," Eloïse said as they went on again, "is nothing – but *nothing!*"

CHAPTER 7

Down at Lake Thun

Jane had already been told that the Chalet School had begun on the shores of the Tiernsee, one of the loveliest lakes in Tirol.

"Then why isn't the school down on the lake-shore now?" she asked instantly.

"Because the Tiernsee is 3,000 ft above sea-level, but here the lakes are right down in the valley and the heat is stifling in the summer," responded José. "That's where it was when Mummy went there, though, and they used to have boating and bathing every day in the summer term and skating in the winter as soon as it was safe."

"I've not done much skating," Jane told her, "but I *can* swim and row. I've surfed at Manly Bay in New South Wales and when we were in New Zealand, Miss Dacre and I were parked at Hokianga Bay and we got plenty of swimming and boating there."

"Lucky you! It's the one thing we miss here. Still, we're better off than the poor things who were at the school when it was at Plas Howell. They hadn't a chance of water sports there."

Most of Jane's swimming and rowing had been by the sea but she soon proved that she was quite capable in lake water. The first trip down had meant less time spent in swimming, as the school, always setting health before everything, had a rule that aquatic sports must begin gradually. Today, they would have longer.

"And that will be a good thing!" Dilys remarked as

they stood on the little platform, waiting for the downward train to reach the Görnetz Platz.

"Here comes the up-train!" Adrienne exclaimed. "See, Jane! Is it not like a beetle climbing up?"

Jane laughed. "It does look exactly like that. Some day, though, I wish they would let us walk down by that path you showed me near the Sanatorium."

"Not in this heat for me, thank you!" José laughed. "We'd melt on the way and they'd have to fetch ice and scrape us on to it to set firm again!"

"Too, too disgusting!" Jane murmured; and José chuckled.

Five minutes later, the down-train arrived and the Middles packed in. It just held them all, so it was as well that no one from the upper shelves was there and they had the three cars to themselves.

When they were settled Dilys reverted to Jane's remarks about Australia.

"I say, Jane, what were you doing in Sydney and New Zealand?" she queried.

"It was during a tour with the Company," Jane explained. "Usually, I lived at the hotel with Mother and Father, but they'd heard there was measles about and as they didn't want any bother about having to isolate me, they sent Miss Dacre and me to Manly while they were touring round New South Wales and Victoria and Queensland. We rejoined them when they had to move to West Australia, but we had a good four months in Manly. I loved it there!"

"But why were they touring?" Adrienne asked.

"And what was the Company?" Sally Godfrey added. "Oh, do you mean that your parents are *actors*? Jane, how miraculous!"

Jane flushed. She had held her tongue about her

parents, partly from shyness, but mainly because she had made up her mind to stand on her own two feet and make no capital out of her famous parents. However, her eagerness over the swimming and boating had made her forget and the secret was out.

"But, darling, of course they are!" she said.

They stared at her and Dilys demanded to know if she was going on the stage, too. Jane laughed ruefully.

"Oh, my poppet, I'd love to, but Father mayn't want me to do it. He says it's the chanciest profession of the lot and the plums are few and far between. You *may* make good; or you may be out for months and months, not earning a penny, and that's not so good."

"But who *is* your father?" José queried.

"William Carew." Despite herself, there was pride in Jane's tones.

"William Carew – do you mean *Sir* William Carew, the big Shakespearian actor?" José exclaimed. "But I've *seen* him! In that film of *Much Ado about Nothing*. He was 'Benedick' and Daphne Cibber was 'Beatrice'. We were in England when it was on in London and Mummy took us to see it. He was simply gorgeous and Beatrice was lovely. We did so enjoy it! Is *he* your dad, Jane?"

"Oh, darling, I'm so glad you enjoyed it so much!" Jane exclaimed. "It was Father's one and only venture on the screen – Mother's, too, for that matter. They've never done another. They both say they prefer the live theatre, though Father agrees that the cinema is really important."

"What was your mother's part?" Adrienne asked eagerly.

"Beatrice; she plays under her maiden name, of course."

"You mean *she's* Daphne Cibber? Gosh!" Dilys gasped. "But why did you never tell us before?"

Jane coloured again. "It didn't seem to matter. And I'd rather have made friends because I'm Jane Carew and not because I'm their daughter," she said. Then she firmly changed the subject. "You know, though I've been to most of the English-speaking countries, this is the first time I've ever been in Switzerland. I do love it! These mountains! They're so beautiful – finer than even the Rockies in some ways, I think. They're grand, of course, but the Alps have something that's all their own. Do you know what I mean?"

"Get your things together, girls," said Miss Ferrars' voice at that moment. "Be sure you leave nothing behind."

They gathered up their possessions in haste and Jane's news was forgotten in the scurry that followed. They left the train, marched in crocodile from the Östbahn to the Schiffbahn on Lake Thun, which meant going along the Hoheweg, Interlaken's main street, and so down to the lake where one of the white lake steamers was waiting at the landing-stage.

Hot as it had been on the Platz, they found it much worse down here, for the two lakes, Thun and Brienz, between which Interlaken stands, are almost completely walled round by the mountains and the place felt like an oven. Once they were out on the water, heading down the lake, however, they were met by a little breeze which cooled them.

Jane glanced round her with beauty-loving eyes that shone. The light wind had little or no effect on the shore-waters and in their glassy surface the mountains were as clearly reflected as in a mirror. Overhead, the intensely-blue sky was cloudless, and she was thankful for her big straw hat which she tilted forward to shield her eyes from the glare of the sun off the water.

This was the quietest part of the day, when even the tourists who throng the lake shores were resting. The girls were, for the most part, content to watch the small towns and villages past which they went, talking little and enjoying the tranquillity of it all. But when they reached the town of Thun and disembarked to march down to the shores and make for their own bathing beach, they chattered hard enough.

The school rented its own beach and on the afternoons when they were there; it was roped off so that they had it to themselves. There were beach huts where they changed and they also had their own big boathouse where their boats were kept. When the Middles arrived, the Seniors were already in the water, swimming, practising diving and life-saving and otherwise disporting themselves. There was a rush for the two big huts allocated to the Middles and in less than five minutes most of them were out again, pulling on their caps and ready and eager for the fun.

Jane was one of the first. She raced across to the water, waded in and was just about to launch out when a hand was laid on her arm. She looked up into Len Maynard's face.

"Half a moment!" Len said. "I know you can swim, but we'd like to see something of your style. Can you bear to give us a few minutes to judge? We want to make a provisional selection this afternoon for the Ste Thérèse team."

"But of course!" Jane was at her most eager. "Only, aren't I rather *young*?"

"Not for the Junior team," Len answered. "We saw you have pace. Now we want to judge style. Over there,

68

please. There are two or three more we have our eye on."

Jane waded along to where three other girls were standing, among them Jack Lambert, Adrienne Didier, whose home was on the Breton coast, and Wanda von Eschenau, daughter of a mother who had excelled at both swimming and rowing in her own school days. Adrienne came to welcome her excitedly.

"Oh, Jane, are they trying you for our team? But how delightful! What strokes do you know? Can you dive?"

Jack paused in her talk with Wanda to listen, her face set in an effort not to scowl. She would never again bait the new girl, but she still could not like her and in her heart of hearts hoped fervently that Jane would not be found good enough to join the team.

"Side-stroke, breast, back, over-arm; and yes, I can dive," Jane said, answering Adrienne. "Duck-dive, swallow, and I have tried double-diving with Miss Dacre."

"Oh, good! I've done all those but double-diving." Adrienne spoke in her own language in her excitement. "It would be delightful if we two were to represent our form, n'est-ce pas?"

Three other girls came splashing up to them – two from Upper IVB and Barbara Hewlett from Lower IVA. Len followed, with Heather Clayton and Ted Grantly, and behind them came half-a-dozen more of the Middles.

"Only Thérèse to come now," Heather said as she surveyed the candidates. "She split her cap when she pulled it on and had to get another from Burnie. Here she comes!" as Thérèse de Grammont raced along the shore to splash into the water as soon as she was near and join up with them.

"Now," said Len, "we've got it all planned out. Ted is swimming out half-way to the raft. You swim out to her breast-stroke. Then change to side-stroke as far as the raft. Wait there for us and we'll tell you what to do next. Line up!"

They lined up; Heather gave the word, and they were off, not without some splashing from one or two before they were fully settled. Ted had already swum out and was clinging to one of the boats, watching keenly as she trod water. Then, having seen them off with Len, she headed for the raft with powerful strokes which took her swiftly past them. Arrived at her goal, she clambered up and stood watching the race.

Jane had settled down at once and it was soon clearly a neck-and-neck struggle between her, Jack and Adrienne and Thyra Lund of Upper IVB. Wanda and Thérèse came a short way behind them and the rest behind those two. Jane reached Heather and the boat half a stroke ahead of Jack but during the second half of the length, Jack overhauled her and grabbed the edge of the raft two seconds before she did, Adrienne following almost at once. They scrambled up and collapsed on it to watch the others. Len came up with the last two, having kept level with them in readiness for any accidents. Heather left her boat as soon as every one was past and reached the raft slightly ahead of them.

"Ready?" she asked when the last girl had been dripping contentedly in the hot sunshine for five minutes. "Right! Line up on that side. There's just room for you all if you're careful – Ted!"

"O.K. I'm off!" And Ted went in with a long, beautiful dive which carried her some distance towards the boat.

"Now," Heather said "dive in and swim overarm as far as the boat. From there, back-stroke, please. Are you ready? Get steady! GO!"

On the word they dived, Jack in such a hurry that she

went in with a wild splash! Let Jane Carew beat her, she would not – not if she could help it! Jane, with no such feeling to upset her, went in cleanly and came up to settle down to the overarm quite a distance away. Adrienne was as good and so were two of the others. Wanda's dive was shorter, but her arms went like pistons and she drew level with the two leaders before they reached the halfway mark and had to change to back-stroke. Jane scored here, for her back-stroke was stronger than either of the others and she went ahead almost at once. Then she was aware of someone fighting to come up with her and a moment later, Jack Lambert was level and the pair had a dingdong race which only ended when Ted shouted, "Stand! and they stood up to their waists in water, panting with their exertions and having made a deadheat of it.

Ted waved them to the shore, but never took her eyes off the other competitors until the last one came splashing in and stood. Then she moved out herself to join her compeers and, while the girls on the beach dried off and got their breath back, the three Seniors gravely consulted together.

Nothing was decided then. It was clear who had both pace and style, but the diving form must be tested, and meanwhile they were sent off to enjoy themselves and make way for the people from St Hilda's.

The recall whistle blew at last and everyone had to come out, dry down and change into fresh swimsuits before tackling the preparation they had with them. Jane lay in the sun, nibbling her biscuits and memorizing the three verses from Tennyson's *Ballad of the Revenge* which she had decided she need not leave since she could memorize quickly. That done, she shut the book, took out her typescript and read the part through carefully and with some amusement.

Priscilla had typed out copies of the play for everyone. Jane read her copy and giggled more than once. For schoolgirls, *The Little Germaine* was quite a good effort, but some of the stage directions stuck her as funny and once or twice she murmured, "Oh, *no!* That's not good theatre!"

"I can learn it all right," she decided when she had come to the end. "It won't take me long to memorize. But I wonder if I dare suggest some alterations. That speech of Germaine's won't do here. It ought to come much earlier. And I'm sure she should begin crying before *this* one."

She knitted her brows as she reread the script. Finally she decided that she had better wait for a rehearsal before she said anything.

"And then only if I can see a good chance," she thought. "It's their play, after all. It's all very well for Father to insist on changes in the script, but I know those girls think I'm only one of the kids."

A shadow fell across her and she looked up to see Eloïse beside her.

"I saw you were reading the play," the Senior said, dropping down on the hot sand beside her. "Think you can manage it?"

"Oh, yes; easily. I could wing through it now after just two readings. It's a very easy part to learn because most of the time the other parts are feeds and you can't go far wrong like that. But I'd like to get it right first," Jane said, looking down at it. "Once you get a sentence wrongly into your mind, it's horribly difficult to correct to the proper lines."

Eloïse gaped at her. Jane's professional phrasing was largely beyond her. However, the kid seemed to think she could do it all right and that, to Eloïse's mind, was

72

the main thing. Two other questions remained. Could she act? And could she sing? Germaine's solo was important to the action.

"You sing, nicht wahr?" the prefect asked.

Jane nodded. "I'm no prima donna, but I can sing all right."

"That is good," Eloïse said with relief. "Tomorrow, we have a rehearsal after Prayers and tonight we will read the play – that is, you may read, but we who know our parts will, of course not use them."

"Thank you," Jane said demurely. She hoped that by that time she would need no script either, but she was wise enough not to say so.

"Then I will leave you now. Memorize all you can, for there is little time left us," Eloïse said, getting to her feet. "Also, tomorrow, we must try your dresses. The length will do but I think you are slimmer than Tina. But we will see." She nodded pleasantly and departed to reassure Priscilla and Ruey about their new Germaine. Jane rolled over on her stomach, propped her chin on her clenched fists and got down to memorizing in good earnest.

CHAPTER 8

Rehearsal

Jane woke early next morning. She had taken her script up to bed with her the previous night, thereby, if she had realized it, breaking a rule. She did not and no one saw what she had done, so she got away with it. She pulled it out from under her pillow after glancing at her watch. She had a good half-hour before the rising-bell sounded and that, she felt, would be quite enough for her to make certain of it. At the rehearsal the night before she had kept the script in her hand, glancing at it from time to time to make sure of certain weak places. The Seniors had been too much absorbed in their own parts to see that she was so nearly word-perfect, but they had been delighted with her rendering of the part.

"If she can *read* it like this," Priscilla said to the rest when Jane had gone, "she ought to be really good, once she knows it thoroughly. Well, thank goodness for that! And thank goodness we shan't need to worry about whether she will be heard or not!"

"No; her diction is really good," Ruey agreed. "Extraordinary for a kid of that age!"

She repeated this to Len Maynard when they met in the Senior commonroom. Len grinned at her.

"Come off it, Rue! Naturally her diction is good! She's spent her whole life with actors whose voices have been properly trained. I'd have been surprised if her own voice were anything but clear and most beautifully pitched."

"Gosh! I hadn't thought of that!" Ruey gasped.

74

"Well, it's all to the good where you folks are concerned. I'm quite looking forward to this show of yours," Len said kindly.

"Welcome, I'm sure!" Ruey bobbed a curtsy. "This condescension of yours overpowers me, lady!"

They both laughed. Then Len added, "By the way, if Jane should give you any hints about the thing, don't jump on her, but consider them carefully. She probably knows a hundred times as much as you folk about plays. Make use of her, my child, and thank heaven for such a gift."

"As you say," Ruey assented. "Certainly we won't jump on her. I'll give the others the tip."

Jane concentrated steadily for twenty minutes. Then she closed the script and tossed it to her bureau. "I know that now! I can't do another thing at it till I get my moves. I do hope it all goes well. They're so keen on it."

She tossed back the bedclothes and scrambled out to go and stand at the wide-open lattice. The view never failed to delight her and now she feasted her eyes on what she could see of the rank on rank of mountains across the valley. The mists must have been heavy, for the grass immediately beneath was hoary with dew and it was not possible to see very far yet; but they were thinning rapidly now. Even as she watched, more and more distant peaks came into sight and she gave a little crow of delight.

"Glorious! I do love this place! If only Mother and Father were here – or near enough for me to see them, I wouldn't ask for another thing!"

The bell rang out, putting an end to her meditations, and she had to strip her bed, say her prayers and be ready to dash to the bathroom the moment the girl before her returned.

Once they were all downstairs most of them made for

the garden, the few who did not going reluctantly to one or other of the practice-rooms to put in some work before Frühstück. Adrienne had gone to her piano, but José and Jean seized on Jane as soon as she appeared and demanded to be told about the play.

"Oh, darlings, I don't think I *can* say anything," Jane said anxiously. "I'll have to ask Ruey or someone first. They mightn't like it."

"Did they tell you not to talk about it?" Jean asked.

"Actually, they didn't, but just the same I'd better keep quiet until I know definitely. Anyhow, wouldn't you rather wait till you see it? More fun that way, I should think."

José made a face. "Perhaps you're right, though I'm dying to know what it's about. OK, Jane, we won't worry you. But mind you're jolly good. You're representing Upper IVB remember!"

"I hadn't thought of that," Jane admitted, "but I'll do my best."

"Have you learned it yet?" Jean asked curiously.

"Goodness, yes! Full rehearsal tonight, you know, and the show itself tomorrow. I wouldn't dare leave it any longer."

"You'll be OK," José said comfortably. "I never knew anyone who learnt by heart as fast as you. When we do rep you seem just to look over it twice and then you know it. Wish *I* could!"

Priscilla came up then. "Hello, folk! Well, Jane, know your part yet?"

"I think so," Jane said.

"Good! Then you've nothing to be afraid of. Eloïse is prompting and she'll help you out if you forget. So will all of us. We all know the thing pretty well off by heart now. So don't get scary. You'll be OK."

Jane deemed it wisest to make no reply. Priscilla patted her shoulder and went off to inform the rest of the cast that at any rate it didn't look as if they would have to worry over Jane Carew getting stage-fright. She was as cool as a cucumber and said she knew the thing.

"Anyone know how Tina is?" she added as an afterthought.

"I asked Nurse before I came down," Gabrielle Ménolles replied. "She is better, but still very weak after all the sickness and pain. Nurse said it had been a bad attack. Tina is to stay in San for two or three days."

"What could have started it?" Thérèse Rambeau wondered. But that, no one could tell her just then.

From VA spent any spare time they had that day wondering how the play would go and whether Jane was sure to be all right on the night. They saw nothing of her for most of the day, since Upper IVB were at work all the morning in the block where the science labs, the geography rooms, art-room and domestic science kitchens were. In the afternoon, Miss Yolland took them out for free sketching and by the time they got back, they had just time to change for the evening before the gong sounded for Kaffee und Kuchen. Nor were the elder girls able to catch their substitute between that and prep, for Jane had unwisely left her drawers in a turmoil and Matey had had a dormitory inspection during the day and sent word that she, Wanda, Kitty Anderson and Renata van Buren must tidy the said drawers as soon as Kaffee and Kuchen were over. The other three were pretty bad, but Jane's was by far the worst and she only managed to finish in time to go in to prep with the rest.

"Mother would call me a regular slut!" she mused sadly as she put her handkerchiefs into their case, wound up loose hair-ribbons and restored the drawers to the pristine order Matey insisted on with everyone. It was not *her* fault if any Chalet School girl was an untidy creature!

However, when Jane went to Hall to join the anxious Seniors, she came in in her usual composed manner and handed over her script to Eloïse.

"Are you sure you can do without it?" Priscilla asked

"If she can, she's the eighth wonder of the world," Mary Allen said gloomily. "Well, we shall see."

They did indeed see. Jane not only went through without the smallest hesitation, but they found that she required little or no direction as to gesture and movement. Her intonation and delivery were excellent and when she very shyly made one or two suggestions – for example, about the crying – they had to admit that she was right.

On her side Jane discovered that while the girls certainly knew their parts and some of them had a real feeling for the stage, they suffered from the usual weakness of amateurs – they failed to be prompt enough on their cues. She herself, with memories of all she had heard from her parents, never made a pause except when it was necessary to the part. Almost before the character who gave her her cue had finished speaking, she was replying. She infected some of the others and by the time they had gone through twice, the action was distinctly quickened to the great advantage of the whole effect. Eloïse timed the second time and as the last line was spoken, she looked up from the book with a sigh of relief.

"We have cut off seven minutes," she told the cast solemnly. "It is still ten minutes too long, but never before have we been able to make it quicker."

"I don't see how we can shorten the time," Ruey said. "We just *can't* cut another thing or some of it won't make sense. I don't see that we can do it any faster even if we *gabble*! Anyone else got any suggestion to make?"

None of the others had and Jane felt shy about making hers. The VA girls were all older and it was *their* play. She liked it, amateurish though it was. It did seem a shame that it should be spoilt by any dragging when she could give them a hint that would certainly help.

Meanwhile, the girls themselves had given it up and turned to another aspect.

"Well, we may be thankful that we have Jane to act Germaine," Marie Lemprière remarked. "You are good, Jane. Truly, you might be the little Germaine herself!"

"But of course," Jane said. "That's what one tries to do."

"How do you mean?" demanded Priscilla. "Explain please!"

"Well, it's just – I've heard my father say that unless you can get into the skin of a part – *be* the person you're playing – you can't hope to do it well."

The big girls looked at each other.

"I see what you mean," Marie said. "We must try to feel as the character feels and think as he thinks."

"That's it!" Jane spoke eagerly. "My father says you should try to know what books he likes – what his hobbies would be – even what food he prefers. You must think as he thinks in every way."

"Gosh!" said Priscilla. "In that case, look out for Gretchen, everyone! If she has to think and feel and have the same tastes as Jules, it's as well it'll be all over by tomorrow night! What an awful creature to have in a decent school!"

The girls laughed. The gifted authors had made Jules, the villain of the piece, almost impossibly evil. Marie, however, who took her acting more seriously than the others, was greatly intrigued.

"I think we have forgotten what a famous actor your

father is, Jane. Can you remember anything he said that would help us?"

Jane nodded, half-shyly. "I'm almost sure he would say that you are not quick enough at picking up your cues," she said.

"How do you mean?" Ruey demanded sharply. "We don't have pauses – not real ones. Or not many, anyhow."

"It's not *pauses*, exactly," Jane said. "But I've heard my father say that the real secret of keeping a play from dragging is for each actor to jump in practically on top of the last word or two of the previous speech."

They thought this over. Mary suddenly dashed across the stage to take up her position for the opening scene.

"Come on!" she cried. "Let's try it out now! First scene, Eloïse. Odette, be ready to come on and do as Jane says – jump right in on top of my last word. Time us, Eloïse!"

They scattered, all eager to try out this technique. They went through the first scene with considerable verve. It didn't always come off, but for at least two-thirds of the speeches it did. When the scene ended, Eloïse exclaimed.

"But this is amazing! Four minutes have been taken off the time!" she cried. "Let us continue and go through the whole play."

"I'm sorry," said a voice from the doorway, "but I'm afraid not. Do you girls realize the time?"

They all swung round to face the Head, who was smiling at them. She pointed at the wall-clock. "Jane should have been upstairs half-an-hour ago and you Seniors must go now. Put those chairs and tables back in their places, please, and then hurry up to the dormitories. Jane, run along at once, dear. Be as quiet as you can so as not to disturb the others. Goodnight, and sleep well."

Jane was off on the word, only pausing to make the

usual curtsy to the Head. The elder girls hurriedly cleared up and set everything in order, ready for the next morning before they scuttled off, too. All the same, it was a jubilant VA that retired to bed that night. The fact that their play had always overrun the time by twenty minutes had worried them. Now, they felt that, thanks to Jane and her father, they could overcome the difficulty.

Said Eloïse to Ruey as they parted at the door of Alpenrose where the latter slept, "I really do think we've found a treasure in Jane Carew."

"So do I," Ruey agreed. "I'm going to the Head for leave to invite Aunt Joey and my cousin Daisy Rosomon, who's with her now, to come and see it and, I may tell you, that's something I shouldn't have cared to do before this!"

She vanished on the last word and Eloïse went on to Leafy dormitory, feeling that if only the whole play could go as that last scene had done, she might even ask Mrs Maynard for advice about writing plays in real earnest.

CHAPTER 9

"The Little Germaine"

"Gosh, but my knees are knocking together!" Ruey Richardson gave a shiver. Then she turned to Jane who was standing in a nearby corner, waiting and ready. "You seem calm enough, young Jane."

"Oh, if you only *knew*!" Jane exclaimed. "Butterflies the size of vampire bats in the tummy, my dear!"

"Some tummy you must have!" Mary Allen remarked. "Tell me, Ruey, have I enough powder on? Eloïse said I was *glistening* and must powder again."

"You look as if you'd dipped your face in the flourbin," Ruey replied frankly. "For goodness' sake wipe some of it off!"

Mary obeyed and carefully removed some of the thick coating of powder on her face. She looked at Jane who nodded. "Oh, my dear, that's *much* better! And that wig's a huge help. Aren't we lucky to have such a gorgeous lot of wigs and stage-props?" she added.

"Oh, we've always done heaps of plays, ever since the school began – and that's twenty-three years ago," Mary said, surveying herself in the mirror. "Where's my knitting? – Oh thanks, Jane! Yes, Eloïse; I'm coming!"

She scurried off, followed by Odette. Left alone, Jane glanced round the dressing room and decided to go too. She could stand in the wings and watch. That would be better than waiting here with that horrible fluttering somewhere in her middle.

"Oh, dear! Mother was right when she told Sylvia

Forbes that it always happened on a first night!" she thought. "Supposing I let them down! How *awful* it would be!"

She slipped into a spare corner behind Eloïse, who was prompting, looking as nervous as any one of the actors. The school orchestra was coming to the end of the gay little composition that had been written as an overture. It ended, and the curtains swung apart to show a chalet living room and the two who opened the play. Jane swallowed hard. Then Phyllis Garstin spoke the first line and the play had begun.

The story was dramatic, not to say melodramatic, and called for dramatic acting. A mountaineer, Aubert, had found a little girl, very ill and in rags, high up in the mountains. Actually, she was the kidnapped daughter of English parents, but had been deserted by her kidnapper to die up there of fever. Aubert had brought her home to his wife, Marie, and widowed mother in their lonely mountain chalet. He and Marie were childless and when they had finally nursed the child back to health and were unable to trace her relatives, they adopted her as their own. Her high fever had robbed her of her memory, so they named her Germaine after the old lady and she became a member of the family.

Jane had little to do in the first scene but lie in the arms of big Gerda Nordheim, muttering from time to time until she was carried out again. Her long fair hair streamed loosely over Gerda's shoulder, for fair hair was a necessity to the plot and VA had made the most of Jane's mane on all occasions. Jane did her best to make herself as light as possible and, luckily for Gerda, it was a short scene.

The next one showed the child recovered and playing the part of daughter of the house. It opened with Aubert saying that though he had done his best, he could find no one who claimed Germaine. Now he felt he must go to the city of Geneva and appeal to the authorities there, for they were in touch with many nations and if the child was a foreigner they could possibly trace her parents. This gave quite a good dramatic opportunity to Odette, the Marie Dubois of the play. Odette was a poor actress, but she could look tragic on the smallest excuse and Priscilla and Eloïse between them had managed to drill some drama into her. Mary, as the old woman, was much better and the audience were quite moved by her pleadings that her son would let things alone and keep Germaine as their own child.

There came the sound of singing outside the window and Germaine passed by it, her hands full of flowers. She came dancing in, still singing, whirled round the room, and finally cast herself into Marie's arms to present her with the flowers.

Jane had a sweet, clear voice and what Tina had made into a mechanical little dance became with her a real joyous whirling, making a striking contrast to Odette's melancholy tones and manner. She broke off to ask why Maman and Gran'mére were so sad. They told her the story of her coming to them and what Aubert meant to do. Instantly, she broke into passionate pleading with him. Why should he? She was happy here and only asked to stay with them. All she could remember of the past was cold and hunger and sickness and a man who shook and struck her if she angered him. The women joined in her pleading and finally Aubert gave in, though he felt sure that one day someone would recognize her by her long fair hair and then there would be serious trouble.

Jane threw herself headlong into Germaine. For the time being she felt as if her very life depended on being allowed to stay with these people and before the scene ended, her eyes were wet with real tears.

Seated in the audience with the Head on one side and Daisy Rosomon, her niece-by-marriage, as they always called it, on the other, Joey Maynard watched her with startled eyes. As the curtain fell amid frantic applause from the girls, she turned and said, "My goodness, Hilda! That child can act all right!"

Miss Annersley nodded. "She can! It was to be expected, of course."

Daisy Rosomon leaned forward to say eagerly, "She'll be going on the stage sooner or later, won't she? She definitely ought to with a gift like that!"

"She may," Hilda Annersley said guardedly. "It will partly depend on her parents. I believe her father would rather she took up a more assured career. But – well, I think fate will prove too strong for him."

"Did Ruey and Co really write this thing themselves?" Joey demanded.

"They did, indeed!"

"You'll have to look to your laurels, Joey," Daisy warned her with a laugh. "They've made quite a job of it."

Joey laughed too. "My good girl, I'm not the only writer this school has turned out. What about Eustacia Benson, for instance?"

"Oh, her!" Daisy sniffed. "I'll grant you she's a learned woman, but for one person who reads her books there must be a thousand who read yours. The curtain's going up again! What happens now?"

The next scene was set two years later. It opened with Germaine singing a song as she moved about, setting the room to rights. Marie entered, helping the old grandmother, now a cripple, and Germaine ran to help too.

From their talk, it became plain that Aubert was absent, guiding a party of climbers and not expected to return till next day. There came a knock at the door. Germaine opened it and a most villainous-looking man staggered in. He wore short breeches and a leather jerkin. One arm he carried inside the jerkin and a leg was tied up with the most gory-looking bandage. He told them that he was Jules Dronier. He had been hunting chamois and had slipped and fallen on his gun which had gone off, wounding him in the leg. He begged for a night's lodging and food.

They agreed instantly and set to work to make him as comfortable as they could, though Germaine, feeling an aversion to him, kept away from him as much as possible. While eating the soup they had brought him, he began to stare hard at her. Presently, he began to ask questions. Was she the only child? How old was she? Had she been born in this mountain chalet?

"And what wonderful hair!" he added, reaching out to one of the pigtails which Jane now wore. She twitched it out of his hand and took refuge beside Gran'mère while he laughed – Gretchen had practised hard at a really sinister laugh and the result was blood-curdling – and inquired when the man of the house would return.

Germaine quickly said that he might return at any time. Meantime, it was growing late and the grandmother must go to rest – all of them must, in fact. They would make him a bed on the settee for the night and perhaps by the morning he would be able to reach a doctor who would attend properly to his hurts. The father would be sure to help him down the mountain and would be sure to return before long – but very soon.

There was a certain fear in Jane's voice which came through her brave words, and the audience were all keyed up when finally Jules was left lying on the settle while the other three went off. As soon as they had gone, he broke into a long soliloquy.

"It must be the same – that hair! Fair and shining and like a cataract! Yet I'll swear she was near death when I left her. How could she survive, ill as she was, and half-starved? I saw to that – Herrgott! Did I not see to it!" Again that horrible laugh came. "I had my revenge then! I wonder how milord and his lady felt when they had my letter, saying I had left their precious only child lying dying on the mountain side? You were clever, there, Jules, my boy! Sending the letter from Spain would put them completely off the track! But all my trouble has been in vain if it is indeed she. How *could* she survive? And yet – that hair! I could never mistake that! Well, if it is she, I must see to it that she disappears at once and forever. So many foreigners visit this country, they might meet her and then would they not know her? He shall never have her back. That I swear! Thanks to him, I wasted seven precious years of my life in one of their English prisons. More, they found the money and jewels, and I had not even that recompense. I swore then he should pay and pay he shall. Let me but heal of my wounds, and then – she vanishes!"

There, the curtain fell and the girls applauded rapturously, though among the two Sixths Maeve Bettany murmured to her cousin Len Maynard, "Don't VA know *yet* that Hamlet soliloquies are a thing of the past? Appallingly out of date I call that effort!"

Here she had to stop, for the refreshments were being handed along – cartons of ice-cream and glasses of iced lemonade, both very welcome on such a warm night as this – and not only among the audience, but behind the scenes too, where the entire cast were congratulating Gretchen and Jane on their work.

"You were the complete villain, Gretchen," Ruey said. "I'd hate to meet you alone in the dark! As for you Jane, you just *are* the little Germaine."

Kirsten Johanssen, a smiling Swede who had brought their share, reported the comments she had already overheard.

"Miss Annersley is delighted and I heard Miss Derwent say to Miss Wilmot that she felt fully repaid for all the hard work she had put in on senior English. And Mlle, too, is quite thrilled."

"Did Aunt Joey say anything?" Ruey asked hopefully.

"Oh, yes, indeed! She said Con was evidently not going to be the only pebble on the literary beach of this school and Eloïse, of course, had inherited gifts from her father. Oh, and Daisy Venables – I mean Rosomon – is there and she said it was long since she had enjoyed any play so much."

"Daisy here?" Ruey exclaimed. "But I didn't know she was coming. Is Laurie there, too – her husband, I mean?"

Kirsten nodded. "Yes; and she said that the babies were all at Freudesheim and we would all see them in due course."

"Oh, blow all that!" Priscilla said impatiently. "You can talk of Daisy and her family any time. What I want to know is if they said anything about Jane?" She glanced round as she spoke, but Jane was nowhere near.

"Oh, everyone is amazed that she is so good," Kirsten returned.

"Well, frankly, I think it's a jolly good thing Tina had that bilious attack," Mary said solemnly. "Oh, I don't mean that I'm not awfully sorry for her," as the rest protested at this. "I am! But you must admit the play wouldn't have gone half so well with her as *Germaine*. She never made half as much of it as Jane has."

"That's true," Ruey agreed. "All the same, it's rotten luck on poor old Tina that she can't even see the thing! – What's that, Pris? Time for the next scene? OK! Here's my glass, Kirsten. Come on, folks!"

The second act went as well as the first. Stated to be three weeks later, it opened with Jules announcing that now he was cured, he meant to seize the opportunity of Aubert's absence from home to inform the Dubois women that Germaine was his own long-lost daughter and he claimed her and would take her home with him the next day.

He did it in a long speech with many gestures, during which Germaine entered with a can of milk and a basket of eggs, both of which she dumped down with some violence when he concluded by trying to pull her to him. She cried that she would not go – she was positive he was lying or why, if he was really her father, did she dislike him so much. She shuddered away from him with such real loathing in her face that Gretchen said later she began to wonder what had made the younger girl detest her so much. Marie flung herself in front of Germaine and defied him to take her, whereupon he suddenly produced a revolver and threatened to kill them all unless they let her go.

At this dramatic moment there came a heavy thud on the door, which opened to show a party of men who explained that they had been climbing the mountain, but had lost their way. They begged for a night's lodging, since it was growing late and would soon be night.

At this point, Jules slipped out by the other door. Marie and old Mme. Dubois poured out their story, helped by Germaine, whereupon the strangers looked round for the villain, but he had vanished. They promised to stay at the chalet until Aubert should return, and guard the trio. They did not think, however, that Jules was likely to return. Marie told them the full story of the finding of Germaine, and one of the strangers, played by Caroline Carlyon, struck his forehead with his fist, exclaiming, "Now I know! It is – it must be the same! You three fellows remain here on guard. I will go at once to the nearest town. We must warn the police. Come to me a moment, little one!"

When Germaine came to him with her face full of wonder, he gripped her shoulders, stared hard at her and then untwisted her pigtails, shaking the mass of hair loose.

"That is the final proof!" he exclaimed. "Madame!" he turned to Marie, who was gaping at him. "I must set off at once, but these others will stay with you. Have no fear! All will be well!" Then he plunged out with such speed that he forgot to lift his feet across the lath of the doorway and nearly fell headlong. Luckily, Aubert was behind and caught and steadied him. The door slammed shut and a moment later he was at the window to say, "Shutter this and *keep* it shuttered. He is a dangerous criminal. I know him now."

"But what of you, M'sieu?" Germaine cried. "If that is so, he may try to kill you. He is armed."

"And so am I!" he lugged a big pistol out of a pocket. "What is more, I am a dead shot and should have no qualms about killing him any more than if he were a lone killer wolf."

He vanished and Germaine stared after him before turning and saying as she pushed the hair off her face, "Somehow, I feel I know him. He is – he is – no; it is of no use. I cannot remember – yet. But I know that I shall and then all will indeed be well."

Curtain!

The final scene took place early the next evening when neither Aubert nor the stranger had returned. The climbers and the Dubois were wondering what had happened that nothing had been heard of their friend. Suddenly Germaine gave a cry and pointed at the open window – still unshuttered.

There stood Jules who had, somewhat surprisingly, exchanged his pistol for a rifle and was aiming it at her through the window.

"Jules – Jules!" she shrieked in a voice of such living terror that Joey Maynard vowed that she nearly sprang on to the stage to the rescue then and there.

Luckily, Jules spoke his final speech in time to prevent her. "I care not what happens to me; but for you, brat, this is your last moment!"

An arm was flung round him at that point, prisoning his arm to his side. The rifle went off with a mild "pop!" Marie shrieked and caught Germaine to her and the men dashed out of the chalet to return a minute later with a positive procession, including Aubert, the stranger and four gendarmes, who hauled Jules along between them. Their leader informed everyone that he was a well-known smuggler who was wanted in more than one country for murder. He would be taken to the nearest prison, there to await trial.

The other three had been tying up their prisoner and now they picked him up and carried him out while the stranger came to Germaine, holding out a photograph and saying, "Germaine, do you remember this?"

Germaine looked at it. Then she gave a cry. "But this is me – and my father and mother. I was just ten when it was done. Oh, and it's all coming back now. I am Joanna Vavasour and I was stolen away by a man who had been my father's valet, only he stole things and was caught and sent to prison. He took me when he came out, many years later. And you, m'sieu, you are my uncle who brought me a beautiful doll from Paris once."

Marie gave a loud cry, and Germaine turned to her with a complete change of expression. "But what about these people who have been so good to me and whom I love so dearly?"

"Don't worry," the stranger said. "My eldest brother is your father. He and your own mother will be coming shortly. I cabled them from the town. When they hear how these kind people rescued you and cared for you, I know they will understand that they too have some claim on you. Madame – Monsieur!" he turned to Marie and Aubert who were standing looking melancholy. "Don't be afraid. Germaine will not be taken from you altogether. My brother and his wife often come to Switzerland for holidays and when they come, they will always bring her to visit you. You will not lose her altogether. Of that I can assure you."

Germaine ran to fling her arms round the weeping Marie. "That is true, I feel sure, for I shall always love you and I shall insist that I spend part of each year with you and I know they will agree. Oh, I am a happy girl, for now I have two fathers and two mothers. And though I may have to be Joanna in England, when I am in Switzerland, where I hope to spend half of each year, I shall always be your little Germaine!"

The curtain fell and thunderous applause arose.

"How that child can act!" Joey said as she clapped vigorously. "All the same, though, it isn't half a bad play, that ending is pure Wardour Street and so I shall tell Ruey when I get hold of her."

"I don't see what else they could have done," Miss

Annersley said, laughing as the curtain rose and the entire cast bowed or curtsied their thanks. "You surely wouldn't want it to end in tragedy with all the principal characters weltering on the floor in their own blood?"

"Well – no-o! That would certainly have cast a damper on everyone. Ha! Now let's shout for – "

But the school was before her. Hall rang with their yells of, "Jane! – We want Jane!" Jane had to come forward to take a call and, to her own amazement, was presented with a box of chocolates from Upper V and a hastily assembled bouquet from Upper IVB who had only thought of it that afternoon and had had to beg flowers from everyone and anyone for the purpose.

"Now the authors!" Nancy Wilmot cried, starting a shout of: "Authors! Authors!" which everyone promptly took up until Eloïse and Priscilla were pushed forward by the rest of the cast, to take a curtain-call which they had not expected.

Miss Annersley glanced at her watch and made a sign to the conductor of the orchestra. Instantly, he was on his rostrum, baton upraised, and as the gifted pair hastened to get behind the curtains, every instrument crashed into a lively march. The play was over.

CHAPTER 10

A Day at Freudesheim

Jane woke on Sunday morning to find that she was no longer just "one of those brats in Upper IVB", to quote certain Seniors. Her own form patted both her and themselves on the back, metaphorically speaking. She had done both herself and the form proud, as they all agreed. In addition, several of Lower IVA congratulated her cordially so long as Jack Lambert was nowhere about. Nor were the Senior Middles behind them. They praised her – sparingly, it is true – and several of them prophesied that if she went on the stage when she was grown-up, she would become a star in short order.

If it had been anyone else but Jane, her head might have swelled alarmingly. She, having been brought up more or less in a theatrical atmosphere, kept hers well screwed on. She had heard snatches of talk about early flowering gifts that came to nothing and she knew a good deal about the difficulties to be met.

"It's too sweet of you to say such nice things to me!" she exclaimed. "Honestly, I haven't done much to deserve them, though – nothing out of the way. In fact," she added ruefully, "if my father had seen me, I rather think he would have had a lot to say."

"I should say he'd have been jolly proud of you," said Ailie Russell who, with her two friends Janice Chester and Judy Willoughby, led the Senior Middles in more than one way. "I can tell you, we all feel you've brought credit to the Middles, and we are pleased!"

94

Seeing Jane looking puzzled, Judy explained. "You see, up to this, when any of our crowd have done anything outstanding, it's not been exactly to our *credit*!" Her hazel eyes danced wickedly. "As a rule when anything specially awful has happened, most folk have blamed *us* for it. I won't say they were always wrong, either."

Janice, a slim, grey-eyed girl with smooth black hair dangling in lengthy plaits over either shoulder, added, "Of course, we *have* rather thought of things to do and done them. But now we're older, we're getting rather sick of always being dropped on for everything!" She sighed in an elderly fashion.

Jane exploded at this. "Oh, darlings, I do so understand! But," she went on, "I don't see how last night's show could count to us. It *was* VA's affair."

The gong summoned them at that point for Frühstück; but Jane went to her place at table with a warm glow in her heart, even though her own sense told her that this was just the uncritical appreciation of girls of more or less her own age.

After the meal, Con Maynard caught her as they were all streaming upstairs to attend to dormitory duties. "Hi, Jane! Half a sec! I've a message for you from my mother. She wants you to come along to tea at Freudesheim this afternoon. And it *is* tea, by the way – not Kaffee und Kuchen. She says bring a friend, anyone you like, and come over about 15.00 hours. She's fixed it with the Head, but it's as well to ask leave, of course." She smiled and went off, leaving Jane startled but pleased.

"Why should Mrs Maynard ask me to tea?" she asked Renata van Buren whose cubicle was next door to hers.

With no Jack there to frown at her, Renata was delighted to explain. "It is what she always does with new girls. Each term she has them as soon as she can so that

95

she may know them. If she had not been in England when term began, you would have been invited before. She's our oldest Old Girl, you know. I've heard her say that she has never really left the school, not even now. When she is at home, she is always in and out and I've heard that sometimes she has even helped with the teaching. You do know she's Josephine M. Bettany, the writer, don't you?"

"Jean told me the first time I went to the library," Jane replied, as she whisked up her pyjamas and folded them.

"There are three babies at Freudesheim, too," Angela Carton chimed in from the far end. "There's Cecil who's four and Geoffrey and Philippa, the twins, who'll be two in June."

"And four more boys besides," Wanda put in. "There are eleven of them."

"Eleven! But my poppet! How *can* Mrs Maynard find time to write books with a family like that?" Jane cried, tucking in sheets and blankets at a great rate.

"Easily, on the whole," said a fresh voice as Len Maynard came in. "Mother always says that having triplets first – Con and Margot and me – got her well into the way of things in the beginning. And then she has Anna, who's been with her since before we were born, and Rösli since we came out here. And, of course, when any of us are at home we lend a hand where it's needed. Have you folk finished yet, for I'm coming to inspect?" She made a rapid tour of the cubicles. "Yes; O.K. Get ready for church, then. Jane, Mother's just rung up to say that you and whoever you're taking are to go over as soon as you've changed back into uniform. The rest of us are going off for the day for rambles and you can't stay here alone. Now hurry up, all of you!"

"May I go and tell José?" Jane asked. "She coming with me."

"Right! Cut along to Daffodil and tell her and then fly to get ready."

Jane went scuttering to find José, who was thrilled when she heard the change in the programme.

"A whole day with Auntie Joey! Scrummy! I've seen nothing of her this term so far. You can't count last night. Auntie Daisy will be there, too, and I haven't seen *her* for years. She lives in England, you see. Right, Jane; I'll be there!"

Jane delayed no more but went to get ready for the morning service. The School had its own chapels, the Catholic one served from the monastery round the shoulder of the mountain and the Church of England one for Protestants where the Protestant chaplain to the Görnetz Sanatorium held services for them each Sunday. The girls were very proud of their chapels, since they themselves had largely helped to collect funds to build both St Mary's and Our Lady of the Snows. The Seniors took it in turns to attend to dusting, sweeping and polishing and providing for the two altars. The school choirs led the singing and at Our Lady of the Snows some of the men employed by the School served at the altar regularly. A certain number of seats in each were allotted to visitors and the nurses from the Sanatorium often cycled over in fine weather, as well as friends and relatives of the patients domiciled near at hand who found it easier to walk to the School's chapels rather than face the three miles which lay between the two establishments.

After service, everyone hurried back across the playing-fields, raced upstairs to change into uniform and then sped down for lemonade and biscuits before they pulled on the big shady hats always worn on hot days as a safeguard against sunstroke, collected their parcels of food and drink, wriggled into their rucksacks and then went out to join up with their own party.

When Jane and José were ready, Miss Derwent, one of the duty mistresses, called them to her, looked them over and then sent them off to Freudesheim. Jack, who had not heard, so far, about Mrs Maynard's invitation, stared after them as they went off.

"Where are *they* going" she demanded of no one in particular.

"To Mrs Maynard's. Didn't you know?" Renata asked.

"No, I didn't!" Jack snapped back. To herself she thought, "Getting her foot in there now, is she?" which was unreasonable of her, since she knew well enough that Joey Maynard had new girls to visit her as soon as she could. But though Jack was firmly resolved never again to resort to bullying, she still disliked Jane Carew with most unchristian fervour.

Jane knew nothing of this and she and José raced gleefully along the narrow path above the sunken rock-garden, through the gate in the dividing hedge, up the slope and out above the rose-garden Joey and Jack Maynard had created some years ago. Here, they found Joey and her babies established beneath a clump of tall firs which provided shade at this time over one corner. Seated beside Joey in the standing hammock was a slight, fair, woman with a baby in her arms, while Joey had a rustic table pulled up at the far end and was busy with long strips of print. In a large play-pen at one side, two curly-headed people were rolling about and a small, black-curled girl of four was sprawled at Joey's feet, intent on a picture-book. The last member of the party was a magnificent St Bernard dog, stretched out at Daisy Rosomon's feet.

As the pair came into sight, Joey was just remarking, "How I do *not* like galley-proofs! Paper eels, wriggling all over the place, drat them!" as she just saved half-a-dozen strips from slipping off the table. "It's no go, Daisy; I'll have to give it up and do them in the study. Galleys and the open air don't exactly agree."

"No one but you would try it on," Daisy remarked as she got up to carry the sleeping baby over to the big pram set at a little distance. "This kid's off at last, so for pity's sake don't make any noise, you folk."

As if in reply, the big dog, who had just winded the visitors, got to his feet with a growl which turned into furious barking. The baby squalled indignantly at the rude awakening; Daisy exclaimed with equal indignation and Joey, casting her proofs on the ground, sprang up and ran across to welcome her guests.

"Come along! Come and join the happy throng! José, you get more like your mother every day. You're the image of her as I first knew her!" She held out her hands as the pair came down the shallow stone steps, caught José and kissed her warmly. "Veta[1] all over again! Just as well, for she tells me young Guita is going to be like your father. Jane, welcome to Freudesheim! This is your first visit here, but not, I hope, your last. Oh, Bruno, *shut up!*" She swung round on the dog. "Friends, old man! And you should know José, anyhow. Come and pat him, Jane. He's more noise than anything else."

Jane went to fondle him and he stopped barking and wagged a flail-like tail at her. The baby, however, continued to yell at the top of excellent lungs.

"It's no use, Joey," Daisy said. "I'll have to take her in. She'll never get to sleep at this rate."

[1] *The Princess of the Chalet School.*

"I told you it wouldn't work," Joey said blandly. "Anyhow, she'll be better in the night-nursery just now. Take her up there and leave her to it. She's tired, poor pet, and she'll soon drop off."

Daisy gave her an indescribable look as she went off, her daughter still howling lustily against her shoulder. Joey looked after her and chuckled.

"Poor old Daisy! Both her boys are sound sleepers, but this latest imp wakes at the least sound. Oh, well, by the time they go to their own place, she'll have got over that, I hope. All mine soon learned to sleep through anything – or almost anything. Had elevenses, you two?"

"Ages ago," José said. "Oh, Auntie Joey, it's lovely to see you again! How Cecil has grown; and the twins too!"

Joey laughed as Cecil scrambled up and came to hold up her face to be kissed. "Haven't they? Jane, this is Cecil, my fifth daughter. And these two are Geoff and Phil, my second batch of twins. Come along and shake hands, you two." She stooped over the play-pen to lift them out and they trotted up to the visitors obediently.

Jane had no experience with tiny children, and when little Phil raised her lips pouted for a kiss, she looked at José before she gave it. Geoff kept back, staring at the visitors with big eyes.

"Hello!" Phil said cheerfully; whereupon her twin seemed to decide that it was all right and followed her example.

"Oh, my dear!" Jane exclaimed. "Can they talk already?"

"After a fashion – and most of the time, I admit," their mother laughed. "That's right, my lambs, but it's goodbye for the present now. Naptime! Come along!"

She held out her hands and they went off with her quite cheerfully.

"How good they are!" Jane cried when they had gone.

José nodded. "Aren't they? But so was Cecil – and still is. Uncle Jack's awfully strict about obeying from the first. He says it's the only way."

"Well, I suppose it is," Jane agreed. "Father and Mother were both strict with me, too." She looked round her. "What a lovely garden, José!"

"Isn't it? But when they first came here, all this was a cabbage patch."[1]

"*What?* But darling, it couldn't be!"

"But it *was!* Auntie Joey and Uncle Jack cleared out the cabbages, had it dug out like this and made a rose garden of it as you see."

"How utterly marvellous! I'd never have believed it! But doesn't Cecil have a nap?" Jane asked, glancing at Cecil who had returned to her picture-book.

"Not now!" Joey had handed over her tinies to Rösli and joined them again. "But she likes one in the afternoon, don't you, Cecil?"

Cecil gave her mother an impish grin, but made no remark.

"I suppose Auntie Daisy put the boys down first?" José said. "Are they here for long, Auntie?"

"Well yes; you might say so. Oh, not in this house. That's only for the next week or two. Then the Rosomon family will be going to their new abode. Know the chalet that Frau Steines had at Ste Cecilie?"

José nodded. "Do you mean they're coming here to live? Is Uncle Laurie joining the San?"

"He is, at long last. He's taking Dr Tyndall's place."

---

[1] *Joey Goes to the Oberland.*

"Mummy will be thrilled when she knows." José suddenly changed the subject. "Auntie Jo, how did you like the play last night?"

"I've seen worse," Joey said solemnly. "I congratulate you, Jane. I'm only sorry your people weren't there to see it. I liked your *Germaine*. You made her come alive. Is this to be your future career?"

"I don't know," Jane said slowly. "I never really thought about it much. I think, though, I'd like it, but I don't know if Father and Mother will agree. I've heard Father say that these days it isn't much of a catch unless you're exceptionally gifted or exceptionally lucky."

Joey thought, though she did not say, that Jane showed every sign of being the first. "Oh, well," she remarked, "there's time enough yet. Only fourteen, aren't you? Then the first thing is to get a decent education and you'll probably be at school for at least three years more. And you won't lack for practice, I may say. We pride ourselves on our plays at the Chalet School." She changed the subject. "And now tell me how you like us."

"Oh, immensely! If only I can pull up enough on my weak subjects to be altogether with Upper IVB by the end of the term, I don't think I could ask any more. But oh, Mrs Maynard, how did *you* like maths?"

"Loathed it. And I drove anyone who had to teach me nearly crackers," Joey said cheerfully. "What about you?"

"I don't mind arithmetic so much and algebra isn't *too* bad. But oh, geometry! I've just got a theorem firmly in my head when Miss Ferrars changes all the letters round and I've had it!"

Joey groaned sympathetically. "How well I know that feeling! What about other subjects?"

"Well, I'd never done any Latin before, but it's easy

so far. I *like* languages. But what I really do loathe is domestic economy. You see, we nearly always live in rooms or hotels and there hasn't been any need for me to learn how to sweep and dust and cook and all that, and it's so *messy*."

"All the same, quite a necessary part of any girl's education. There may come a time when you have an ordinary home and then you'll be very glad that you can manage it properly. And believe me, you *will!* Frau Mieders is a dear, but she's awfully thorough."

"Oh, she's a poppet!" Jane agreed.

"Mummy always says she's glad she had to learn," José chimed in. "When they had to escape from Belsornia[1] and I was a tiny baby, she was thankful that she'd had to learn housekeepery things so that she could do them. I don't mind it too much myself and I love cooking. It's fun mixing a whole lot of things together and seeing them turn into a luscious pudding or a cake that melts in your mouth!"

Joey laughed. "I like cooking myself, although," she added with a twinkle, "I won't say that *all* my efforts have turned out 'luscious'. You ask Daisy about my original fillings for sandwiches for our house-warming here!"

She refused to say any more, though they both teased her. She went off presently to attend to her duties and the schoolgirls were left to amuse themselves. Cecil was still occupied with her book.

"Do you think you *will* be an actress?" José asked.

"I don't know. I'd love it for some things," Jane said thoughtfully, pressing a forefinger into the pretty cleft of her chin. "What about you? What are you going to do?"

"I'm not sure. I'll have to do something. We haven't a

---

[1] *Highland Twins and the Chalet School.*

lot of money in our family and there are Freddy and Carl as well as the two kids who come after me. Freddy's doing engineering and Carl wants to be a doctor and that means a long training. I'd like to be a barrister, really, but there again, you have to be lucky or it means hanging on for ages before you do really well and Mummy couldn't afford me much of an allowance."

"But what does your father say?" Jane queried.

"Papa was killed in a flying accident when I was only a kid like Cecil. He was the Duc di Mirolano and Mummy is really the ex-Crown Princess of Belsornia.[1] Only the Reds have snaffled the country, so we haven't to bother about being royal, thank goodness!"

Jane gasped. "But darling! This is news to me!"

José grinned. "I thought it would be. Grandpapa is ex-king of Belsornia but he has a cattle-run in Australia now. He doesn't know much about it, but his partner does. That," she added frankly, "is why Carl can do the doctor-job. Grandpapa will pay for his training."

"But do listen, José! Isn't your name Helston?"

"Papa's family name. Mummy and he said they weren't going to be displaced royalty if they could help it. There's an underground party in Belsornia who hope that some day we'll all go back; but I doubt it. The boys and I don't want it either. Anyhow, till it comes, we're forgetting it. And don't chat about it, please. Not many people at school know and I don't want them to. I'd rather make my own way as José Helston."

Jane could understand that. It was her own feeling with regard to her famous parents. She promised to say nothing and as Joey came back at this point and began to talk of the annual Sale in aid of the Sanatorium, the subject

[1] *Highland Twins and the Chalet School.*

dropped. The Chalet School, Jane decided, had so many interests going on that you really had little or no time for outside things.

"Just the same," she said to herself when she was in bed that night, "José's air of being Somebody is explained. She never puts on frills, but you can't help feeling that she is absolutely sure of herself. Is that what I mean? I think so, though I never bothered to think about people like this before. It's coming to school, I suppose. I was an awful baby when I first came – just took everyone and everything for granted. But even in this short time I've begun to think. I suppose I must be ageing!"

The aged party turned over once more and fell asleep with a last thought of how interested her parents would be to meet some of these girls. She hoped that when the tour ended they would come to Switzerland for a holiday during termtime and get to know them. But that could not be for a long time yet.

CHAPTER 11

A Battle Royal

"Well, it's been a peaceful week for once!" Maeve Bettany stretched, and grinned at her triplet cousins with whom she was having a quiet chat. It rarely happened, for Maeve, as Head Girl, had plenty of work apart from various lectures in school hours, and the Maynard triplets as they grew up had begun to have widely differing interests. This meant that at school they saw less of each other than they had done previously. However, all four had a free period just then and had foregathered. Maeve was leaving school at the end of term. She would have two months holiday at home and then was to join a big touring agency to train as a lady courier.

"Shall you like being always off somewhere?" Con asked.

Maeve nodded. "It's exactly my cup of tea. My languages are good enough to pass muster, thank goodness! I can speak French, German and Italian with fair fluency and I'm coming on in Spanish."

"*And* you'll be able to spread yourself, organising trips and so on," Margot chimed in.

"Yes; that, too. I like organising and seeing that everything goes smoothly. I'm quite looking forward to it."

"Well, things have gone smoothly enough this week," Len commented. "Even young Jack seems to have piped down considerably. I'm thankful about that, Jack was getting a good deal more of a problem than I enjoy."

"The fruits of growing up, I expect," Maeve said half

laughing. "It takes some girls more violently than others, I believe."

"I never saw that it took *you* violently – or any of us three, for that matter." Con looked at them with serious brown eyes.

"That's all you know!" Margot's fair face was flushed.

"You *were* a bit of a nuisance a couple of years ago,"[1] Maeve agreed, "but you grew out of it. Jack will do the same. And after all, she can't expect to have things go her way every time. Neither can Jane. They've got across each other somehow. They'll just have to snap out of it. That's all! Though I'm bound to add that most of the trouble seems to have come from Jack. Jane appears to be peaceable enough, taking her on the whole. Jack's much more – well, I hesitate to call her violent, but you know what I mean."

"Jane's more grown-up – on the outside, at any rate," Len decided. "I couldn't say what she's like underneath that gay exterior of hers."

"Oh, I should say she was jolly enough," Margot said lazily. Then she sat up with so little regard for the fact that she was in a hammock that it turned over completely and shot her out on to the grass.

"What's biting you?" Maeve began; but she got no further, for a bunch of girls from Lower IVA came hurtling round the end of the shrubbery at that moment, and flung themselves on Maeve and Len – Con was hauling Margot to her feet.

"Oh, Maeve, come at once!" they shrieked. "Len, come and stop Jack and Jane fighting!"

As they all shouted at once, it was difficult to make them out. Maeve silenced them with a sharp, "Be quiet,

[1] *Theodora and the Chalet School.*

all of you! Now – *you*, Barbara! What is all this in aid of?"

Looking half scared, half inclined to giggle, Barbara gasped, "It's Jane and Jack. Jack's pulling Jane's hair and Jane's – trying to stop her."

"Where?" Len demanded quickly.

"In the garage yard. It was Ferry's car. Jane was washing it down and Jack saw her and tried to – well – to stop her."

"And they won't stop," Carmela Valenti put in. "We've tried to make them–"

"But they wouldn't listen to us," Celia Everett finished the story, "so we came to find someone who could – only not a mistress if we could help it."

"Drat the little nuisances!" Margot spoke with fervour as she dusted off her hands; but Maeve and Len had already set off at a run to put a stop to whatever was going on.

The garage yard was at the back of the main building, which accounted for the fact that no one in authority had heard the mêlée, though as the two big girls rounded the block the noise made them redouble their speed.

"If the Head hears this–" Maeve found breath to pant.

Len said nothing, but shot ahead. The next minute she came on a scene that made her wonder why no one else *had* heard. In the middle of the yard stood the little runabout which belonged jointly to Miss Ferrars and Miss Wilmot. Part of it was gleaming wetly; the rest was mud-splashed. A bucket half-full of clean water stood at one side; close to it, another had rolled into the long gutter and beside it was the big car-sponge. A mob of excited Junior Middles was clustered in front of the garage doors and beside the car were Jane and Jack – and a pleasaant vision they made! Jane's blue frock was splashed to the

108

neck with muddy water. Her face was white and her eyes gleamed like pieces of steel. She was clutching one long plait with her left hand while with her right she seemed to be trying to push Jack's chin skywards. Jack was crimson; she was hauling at the plait she gripped as if she meant to yank the hair out by main force. With her free hand, she was trying to shove Jane aside.

Maeve reached them before Len could do more than open her mouth. She proved her capabilities on the instant. "Be *silent!*" she shouted to the milling spectators who stopped yelling with stunning suddenness. "Jack – Jane! Stop this disgraceful behaviour at once – *at once*, do you hear!"

"She's pinched my job!" Jack gasped, not ceasing to yank. "The – the–" Len clapped a hand over her mouth, cutting her short. Con and Margot, who had arrived by this time, rushed forward and helped to pull the combatants apart, each holding one of the fighters firmly, once they were separated. Jane's eyes were full of tears from pain and she lifted one grimy hand to rub them clear. Jack tried to struggle free, but Con's hands were firmly on her shoulders with all Con's weight behind them, and she found it impossible.

Maeve took advantage of the silence. "You little girls may go *quietly* to the tennis courts and stay there until I send for you," she said, glaring at the pack, who looked uncommonly subdued now that there was someone in authority to take charge. "Go with them, Margot, and see that they sit still. Len, you take Jane and fetch her along to my study. I'll help you with Jack, Con." And she took one of Jack's arms in a firm grip. Con took the other and between them they marched off the recalcitrant Jack, who fought every inch of the way. For the time being, she really had lost her head.

Len had no trouble with Jane in that way, though the look on that young person's face warned the prefect that they were going to have trouble with her. Jack might have the more violent temper, but Jane, when fully roused, was clearly quite as obstinate and unforgiving.

Arrived in the study, Len shut the door and, for good measure, turned the key. Jack looked as if she might make a dive to escape at the first chance. Maeve sat down in her wicker chair, Len perched on the window sill and Con took up a position behind the culprits, who had been placed behind the table.

Maeve looked the pair over judicially and in silence. "Yes," she said at last. "I think the first thing is to make them clean and tidy. Len, take Jane along and see to her, will you? Jack can wait till you come back."

Con unlocked the door and Jane was marched off, first to a bathroom where Len saw to it that she scrubbed herself clean; then to her cubicle where she had to change – she was wet to the skin – brush out her hair and replait it, and finally carry her wet clothes along to the laundry-chute where they would be collected next day by one of the laundry-maids. Then, still in dead silence, Len marched her charge back to the study where they walked into an icy atmosphere of disapproval.

By this time, Jack was coming to her senses. She was standing by the table with a hangdog air and even when Jane came in with Len, she kept her eyes on the floor. Con stood up, touching her on the shoulder with the brief command, "Come along!"

Jack went with a severe-looking Con, to return very clean, very neat and very sheepish. Con set her down on the short form Len had brought in. Then she joined Len and Maeve at the other side of the table and there was a painful silence.

Maeve broke it at last, just as Jane was beginning to feel that she must yell if it went on. "Yes; you certainly *look* better."

Even her cousins were startled by her tone. But Maeve had determined to put a stop to this sort of thing at once. It was not the first time Jack had tussled with another girl and the prefect felt it was more than time that she stopped babyish behaviour of this kind.

"I wish to know," she said icily, "what was the meaning of your outrageous behaviour just now. Which of you began it?"

There was no reply. Her question had reminded Jack of her many grievances and Jane was telling no tales. Maeve waited. Then she changed her tactics.

"Jane, did you begin it?"

Jane set her lips and looked at the toes of her sandals. Seeing there was nothing to be gained there, Maeve repeated the query to Jack.

"She was taking on *my* job. I *always* see to Ferry's car!" Jack growled.

"Miss Ferrars, if you please!" Maeve's voice sent a shiver down Jane's spine, but Jack, with steadily rising wrath, refused to be impressed.

"It's my job! I always do it – everyone knows–"

"Thank you; that will do. It was you who started it."

Jack gave an inarticulate growl.

Maeve ignored her and turned to Jane. "Why did you start in on the car?"

"Miss Ferrars asked me. I couldn't exactly refuse," Jane said sulkily. Her head was still sore from Jack's determined efforts at scalping her and though it took a good deal to rouse her temper, once roused it was not so easily calmed.

"You could have refused all right!" Jack snarled at her. "You know well enough that it's *my* job!"

"But I didn't!" Jane retorted swiftly. "And even if I had, I couldn't have refused when I was asked flat like that."

"What, exactly, did Miss Ferrars say?" Maeve inquired. Most of her sympathies were with Jane, so she was determined not to let Jack miss the smallest advantage.

Repeating it like an exercise, Jane replied. "She said, 'If you're not doing anything else, Jane, I wonder if you would mind wiping over my car with water and a sponge? Miss Wilmot and I want her later on, and she's more than a little muddy.' And," added Jane resentfully, "just how I could say 'No, I won't!' or 'Get someone else!' is more than I can see."

"No; not you!" Jack was seething again. "You sneaked my cubey and now you're trying to sneak my special job!"

"I'm not! I couldn't care less–"

Jane was interrupted by Maeve banging the table so violently that her fingers stung. "That will do! You two are not here to continue your quarrel. Jack, if you speak another word until I give you leave, you'll go straight to the Head!"

With a sudden memory of what had happened the last time she had been sent, Jack was silent at once. Maeve gave her an intimidating glare and turned to Jane.

"Has no one told you that Jack generally does help Miss Ferrars and Miss Wilmot with their car?"

"No one ever said a word to me about it. How could I know?" Jane said sulkily.

"I see. Well, Jack?"

"I don't believe it!" Jack growled.

Jane flushed, but after what had happened to Jack, she dare not speak. Maeve gave them an exasperated look.

She could willingly have shaken the pair till their teeth rattled, but that would do no good. She controlled her own mounting temper with an effort and looked at Len.

Len took the hint. "Jack! Do you remember what happened during your first term here?"[1] she asked.

Jack stared at her. Then she remembered. She had insisted that she had not been responsible for a shock that Miss Andrews had had and no one had believed her – or only very few. She had raged about it, but it was not until another mistress had explained that she had been the innocent cause of what looked like an unpleasant trick that the other girls had realised that Jack had been telling the truth and stopped ostracizing her as a liar.

"I – I – yes," she got out. Further, she would not go.

Len was relentless. "Then you also remember how you felt when no one would believe your word?"

Jack twiddled her fingers, but finally gave a jerky nod.

"Then," said the prefect, still in that gentle, rather cool voice, "what right have you to assume that Jane is lying now?"

"I always tell the truth!" Jack said proudly.

"So, I expect, does Jane. Well?"

Jack darted a look at her, but Len was inflexible. "*Well?*" she repeated.

Jack remained obdurate and Jane, once more roused by her attitude, broke in.

"I don't tell lies!" she cried. "I don't care what Jack Lambert may think, but what I said was true – true – *true!*"

"I see it was," Maeve said abruptly, for Jane's tone carried conviction. "Very well, Jane. We believe you. At the same time, you had no business to fight as you did.

---

[1] *Leader in the Chalet School.*

You're neither a schoolboy nor a baby. You're fourteen and expected to behave like fourteen. The fact that it was clearly Jack who began it makes it a little less serious, but in future, keep your hands to yourself. Now you may go. Take your book and go and sit by yourself in the arbour and stay there till the bell goes. Perhaps, by that time, you will have learned that a girl who may be a full Senior Middle next term can't behave in that way. Yes; go!" for Jane had made no effort to move.

Con slipped an arm through hers and hauled her to her feet. "Off with you!" she said. "Be thankful this hasn't meant a Head's Report!" She opened the door and Jane stumbled out thankfully. Between her sore head and her equally sore mind, she felt as if her world had been turned head over heels. As she went, she made up her mind to give Jack Lambert the widest berth she could for the future. Horrible, *horrible* girl!

"I wish I'd never–" Jane thought; then she caught herself up. *That* wasn't true. She loved the school. Jack was the only real snag and one girl wasn't going to make Jane Carew miserable – not if she knew it! Jane tossed her head and went to obey Maeve's final command.

Meanwhile, in the study, the Seniors were facing a sticky situation. Jack had a hot temper. She had nursed her grievance against Jane all the term and this car business had been the last straw. In many ways more like a boy than a girl, she was happiest when she was fiddling with machinery. At home she and her father had spent many a happy Saturday up to the arms in grease and dirt. Her first term at school had been difficult partly because she was deprived of her favourite ploy. Then the understanding Miss Ferrars had proposed that she should help to look after her car and it had made all the difference. When she had come racing round the corner of the

114

garages and seen Jane Carew at work on her own special charge, it had been too much for her. The result had been the rough-and-tumble to which the horrified Junior Middles, finding themselves unable to cope, had called the prefects.

Not that Jack breathed a word of all this to them. Indeed, it was not until Maeve had finally summoned Barbara Hewlett and got a fairly straight story from her that anyone could make much sense of it.

Having heard Barbara out and dismissed her, Maeve sent Jack off to cool her heels in a nearby room with Con on guard and took counsel with Len.

"You're the one who seems to be able to manage the young pest best. What do you advise?"

"What about going to Ferry and Willie about it? We don't want to give the little ass another Head's Report or heaven knows what sort of term-report she'll take home. It's mad, of course, but where Jane Carew is concerned, Jack doesn't seem to be able to see straight. Those two are jolly understanding and they might be able to help us. Anyhow," Len added, "in the beginning, it was Ferry's fault for wishing that job on to Jane. She ought to know Jack by this time!"

"It's quite an idea. Right! But what do we do with Jack while we hunt Ferry up?"

"Leave her where she is with Con. It won't hurt her to be alone for a little to think things over. Probably by the time we come back, she'll have cooled down and be more ready to listen to reason. There's one thing about Jack. She flares up like a volcano, but I've never known her hold a grudge for any length of time. I suppose," Len added in an elderly way, "it's the result of having to begin to grow up. She isn't a kid and she isn't – well – mature, and she doesn't know what to make of herself."

" 'Youth is a good age, but fussy,' in short," Maeve quoted, laughing. "All right! Better let Con know what's happening, though."

"Right! You go on to the staff room and I'll have a word with Con and follow."

The two mistresses were easily found and, mercifully, were alone in the staff room. They listened to what Maeve and Len had to say. Then they looked at each other.

"I'd better deal with it myself," Miss Ferrars said rising. "I'm sorry it's happened, but I was told that the whole of Lower IVA were at extra art as a punishment for bad behaviour during their lesson. Jane was wandering round by herself, and we wanted the car as we have to get off early to Berne so I just asked her to wipe it over. I do apologise, Maeve."

"I don't see why you should," Maeve said. "Jack knows well enough that you *don't* behave like a hooligan, whatever may happen. She had no right to go for Jane like that and so far as I can gather, Jane's share was mainly self-defence. I've ticked her off and I don't think we need do anything more about her. But Jack's a complete pain in the neck!"

"Oh, she's a regular stormy petrel," Miss Wilmot said. "She'll steady down as she gets older, I expect. Don't worry, you two. You seem to have dealt with the affair quite wisely. Miss Ferrars will go and talk to the monkey – where is she, by the way?"

"In that little room next door to my study, with Con on guard."

"Right! Skip off and deal with her, Kathy. OK, you two. We'll cope now."

Thankfully, the prefects left it in her hands. Just what the two mistresses said to Jack, only they and that criminal ever knew. It was effective, all right. Before bedtime

116

Jack, looking sheepish, came to apologize to Maeve and announced that she had told Jane she was sorry for pulling her hair. But when this was over, she stalked off. She might have had to beg Jane's pardon and she supposed, after what Ferry had said, that it hadn't really been her fault this time, but never, as long as she lived, would she like Jane Carew!

CHAPTER 12

Smallpox – and Half Term

"I'm glad," said Kathy Ferrars in the staffroom next day, "that those girls had the sense to come to Nancy and me and did *not* bother the Head. She's got quite worry enough as it is!"

"She certainly has," Miss Derwent agreed. "How on earth can it have started up, anyone? I thought smallpox was a thing of the past."

"Not in eastern countries," Miss Moore, head of the geography, reminded her.

"No; that's true, of course. Oh, well, I don't see that we need worry up here. When are the doctors coming to perform the awful operation?"

"This afternoon," Matey informed them. "Five-sixths of the School seem never to have been vaccinated since babyhood, so they'll be hard worked."

"The School or the doctors?" Nancy Wilmot queried with a grin.

"You know perfectly well what I mean," Matey said with dignity. "What I want to impress on everyone here is to keep an eye open for anyone who seems off-colour and report her at once. And that goes for all of you as well as for the girls."

"It's a sickening nuisance with half-term so close," Miss Bertram remarked. "This means no going home, of course."

"It also means no expeditions," Miss Moore added.

[1]"This sort of thing happened once before," Miss Wilson, who had come from St Mildred's to visit them, remarked reminiscently. She glanced round the crowded room where they were assembled for coffee, since a fine rain was falling. "Do you remember, Anna? And you, Jeanne?"

"I heard of it," Mlle replied, leaving the coffee-pot to take care of itself and coming to join in the gossip. "I was absent that term, as you may remember."

"You and Hilda and Teddy. I did manage to get back after the frantic letter I had from Jo. Yes, I remember. Well, the whole school was quarantined with german measles that half-term and we had to entertain them somehow. We managed, too." She chuckled.

All those who had been at the School during that memorable term joined in her chuckles.

"What did you do?" Nancy asked wistfully.

"Dozens of things! Among others, we revived our 'Mrs Jarley's Waxworks'."

"Wish I'd been there to see you! I've heard of your first effort."

"We might try it again if we have a wet day," Kathy Ferrars suggested.

"It *would* be fun! I remember that 'Mrs Jarley'. I was in IVA at the time and I remember laughing till I was nearly sick," Rosalind Yolland said.

Kathy Ferrar swung round on her. "Yes; and that reminds me! What *is* all this about Lower IVA having extra art for bad behaviour?"

"It didn't come off, for they came and apologized to me in fullest form and when I heard just *why* it had happened, I was thankful to clear them out and enjoy my

---

[1] *Gay from China*.

laugh in peace. What happened? Anna, it began in one of your classes, actually." She laughed across at Frau Mieders, who also laughed.

"But it was terrible!" she exclaimed. "I was teaching them to make polishes and they were mixing furniture polish. I was called to the telephone halfway through the lesson. Truly, I was not away more than five minutes, but in that time, they had used all the turpentine I had given them. Someone suggested that they might use paraffin to – to – ah! I know! – to eke it out. To whom the fault was I could not discover, but the paraffin can was full and Val Gardiner and Celia Everett spilt it all – but *all* – over themselves and the table and the floor and all the silver they had already polished. The smell was terrible and for Val and Celia, I had to wash even their hair. Though how paraffin in their hair they got, I cannot tell!"

"I see! Well, *I* knew nothing about it, and I'd set up a still-life study for them to draw consisting of a duster, a brush and a *paraffin-can!*' Rosalind stopped, for by this time the others were in fits of laughter. "It seems, Anna," she resumed when she could be heard again, "that in your fury you muddled up your French and said some quite surprising things, and between that and the way those young imps looked *and* my can, it was too much for them. They all doubled up and you never heard such a noise! Naturally, I was annoyed and I condemned them to sitting still for the whole lesson and coming back later in their free time to make it up. However, as I said, I got a most abject apology from them and forgave them."

"I see! Well, what with one thing and another, you upset that crowd to the extent of Jack Lambert and Jane Carew having a stand-up fight – though I can't say I blame Jane. She seems to have acted in self-defence."

"Let's hope that having to stay put during the whole of

half-term doesn't cause any more battles!" Miss Derwent murmured.

"Any casualties?" Miss Wilson inquired.

"Jack's been limping about – I think she banged her knee and bruised it badly. And Jane had to go to bed early with a bad headache," Miss Bertram said.

"So that's the reason!" Matey said darkly. "They didn't tell *me*. Let's hope they've learnt a lesson!"

"When's the half-term notice going up?" Miss Andrews queried.

"Not till later next week, I believe. No need to ask for trouble before we must!"

The girls were also asking the same question. That week passed and no one had even hinted at what was to come. Two or three people whose vaccination had "taken' badly, didn't care. The rest did. The Seniors were sure that there could be no going away this term, but the Middles and Juniors were still hopeful.

"Deney's awfully *late* with the lists!" Dilys Edwards complained when the weekend had passed and they were still without information.

"We have been told that we shall have no trips to other places," Marie Bellever sighed. "I do not like it at all, me. I had hoped to have the long weekend chez-nous, but since this morning when Mlle told us that it was impossible, I have tried not to think of it. Hélas! I had so anticipated it!"

That was on the Tuesday. The final blow fell next day. Prayers over and the Catholic girls seated in Hall in their places, the Head rose from her seat, where she had been talking in a low voice with some of the mistresses, and came to stand at the lectern.

"I am very sorry, girls," she said, her beautiful voice reaching clearly to all parts of Hall, "but though you have

121

been told that there can be no going home for anyone this half-term, I know many of you have been hoping for expeditions at least. Now I must tell you that even expeditions are off for the present. It was hoped at first that the cases of smallpox reported from various cities and towns would prove to be isolated ones. Last night, it was clear that they were not. One or two of the big cities have as many as eighty cases and it seems to be spreading everywhere. So far, thank God, there are none up here. All precautions are being taken to ensure that none occur. That means that we are tied to this shelf until it has ended. Unless any cases occur, you will be free of the entire shelf. If any do, it means being tied down to our own grounds. However, until it happens, we won't worry about it. But you can guess what this means. We can't even go down to Interlaken." She paused amid groans from the listening girls.

"What *rotten* luck!" Jack muttered to Gillie who was sitting next to her. "I was hoping we'd go to Lucerne this time. There are some jolly big engineering works there and I hoped we might visit them."

"Dry up!" Gillie hissed back. "Andy has her eye on us!"

Jack promptly "dried up" and Miss Andrews, who had been glaring at them, transferred her gaze to Arda Peik and Renata van Buren whose heads were suspiciously close together.

The Head was speaking again. "I know; and I'm as sorry as you. However! At least we don't have to worry here. Everyone is either immune or has been immunized; but it's wiser to be safe than sorry. Also, please remember that you are to visit no one without permission, even up here."

"Not even home?" Len Maynard stood up to ask.

"Well, we are so much one with Freudesheim that we have decided that it may count with the school. All other houses are forbidden, though."

"What about letters, please?" It was Monica Garstin, Head of the St Hilda girls, who had risen to ask this.

"All letters, whether coming to or going from here, will be disinfected before distribution. That will be all right, Monica."

Monica looked relieved as she sat down. Mrs Garstin had not been well lately and the three Garstin girls were all anxious for news from home.

"Now," said Miss Annersley, "I have one other command to lay on you. If anyone feels at all seedy, she is to report at once to Nurse. And though I expect you are all feeling upset about this, cheer up! You can trust us," she half-turned to the Staff as she spoke, "to see that you have as jolly a time as possible. Various notices will go up on the notice-board from time to time, so keep your eyes open. That is all just now. School – stand! Turn! Forward – march!"

Miss Lawrence, head of the music staff, swung round to the piano and struck up a gay march and they marched off smartly to attend to morning duties before going to their form rooms to prepare for work.

No notices appeared on the board that morning nor in the afternoon. Miss Dene was too busy with her multifarious duties to attend to them. But as soon as prep was over and they were free, Upper IVB and Lower IVA and B made a beeline straight for Hall and clustered round the big notice-board which was filled now.

Half-term began at the end of morning school on Friday and went on till Tuesday evening. With practically five days to be filled, the girls had spent a good deal of their time wondering what they would do. Even now they were not sure. Outdoor fun had been planned for each day, but every notice began, "Weather permitting". Saturday evening was to bring "Mrs Jarley's Waxworks Show", given by the staff in Hall.

"What's that?" Jack demanded.

"Goodness knows, but it sounds good," Gillie said. "On Friday we finish work at Break and then go off for a ramble! Smashing!"

"Better not let anyone hear you using *that*!" Jean Abbott said warningly.

Gillie made a face at her. "Sez you! Oh, all right! I'll say 'nifty'. Will that suit you any better?"

Jean grinned. "It doesn't really matter to me, but don't forget we have our Sale coming along presently. You won't be able to buy much if all your pocket-money has gone in fines."

"Oh, glorianna! I forgot the Sale! Better be careful, I suppose. I do wish people weren't so *fussy* about what you say!"

All the same, Jean's warning reminded a number of people of the school's rule. A certain amount of slang had always been permitted, but there were words and expressions which definitely were not, and "smashing' was one of them. In any case, the next thing was to find out which was your party for a ramble and they all hunted through the lists eagerly.

Jane discovered that she was with Jean, Dilys, Sally, José and Adrienne, all friends of hers. Jack and her gang formed part of the group, and for good measure, Celia Everett, her elder sister Audrey, who was a shining light of Vb, and Audrey's special friends, Enid Matthews and Mélanie Lucas. The Seniors were represented by the three Maynards, Ruey Richardson, and a pair of friends from VIb, Alicia Leonard, a prefect, and Betty Landon who was noted as being one of the most inquisitive girls who had ever entered the school.

"Gosh! What a mixed bag!" Margot Maynard said later when the two most senior forms took an opportunity to survey the board. "Oh, well, we've got Willie and Ferry, so no complaints!"

Friday dawned with every sign of a scorching day to come. The mists lay heavily everywhere early in the morning, but by the time the girls sat down to a holiday Frühstück of freshly baked rolls, hot from the oven, dishes of fruit after scrambled eggs, and delicious café-au-lait to top up, the mists were beginning to crawl away and the mountains across the valley loomed up clearer and clearer.

Joey Maynard had sent a special invitation to Felicity, her fourth girl, to spend the day at Freudesheim and bring any friends she liked with her. She may have regretted her lavish invitation when Felicity arrived with rather more than half her form. Or, being Joey, she may not. The triplets were to go on Sunday with *their* friends, but besides that, Joey had given some thought to what to do if the weather turned nasty and, while Felicity and the others were enjoying themselves in the garden, she was upstairs in a room not in general use, working for dear life.

At School, the girls began to assemble in their parties, each wearing her big hat and with her rucksack on her back. All the food and drink went in separate baskets which they carried between them, but the rucksacks were crammed with kodaks, painting materials, needlework and knitting, storybooks, writing-cases, fruit and sweets.

To Jane's party came Miss Wilmot and Miss Ferrars, likewise bearing rucksacks, but Miss Wilmot's contained the first-aid case without which Matey allowed no group to go from School on a day's outing. Miss Ferrars had a case of sewing-cottons, needles and scissors in case of accidents to clothes. Later, much later, both were thankful to have them.

"The long and the short of it!" Margot giggled in an undertone to Con, who joined in the giggle. "Aren't they a contrast!"

They were. Miss Wilmot was both tall and broad while Miss Ferrars was on a miniature scale. But there was more to it than that. Nancy Wilmot was fair with blue eyes and honey-coloured hair glinting under her big hat. Kathy Ferrars was brown-eyed, brown-haired and brown-skinned. Nancy was a placid, happy-go-lucky creature, though she could be as icily dignified as anyone when she chose. Kathy was quick in movement, thought and temper. Both were great favourites with the girls and more than one of the other clumps cast envious looks after them as they set off along the highroad, making for the firwoods and the stream which flowed through them to end by flinging itself over the edge of the shelf, tumbling down to join the river flowing far, far down in the valley.

"Croc until we leave the Platz," Miss Wilmot said. "After that, you may break. Here are a few 'don'ts'. Don't rouse the neighbourhood. Don't fall over the edge; we want to take you all home entire. Don't remove your hats until we're well up in the woods. Matey would hate us if we took a dozen sunstroke cases back for her and Nurse to cope with!"

The girls went into fits of laughter at this. When they were quiet, she added to her diatribe. "One 'do.' *Do* enjoy yourselves. Now lead on, Jack and Gillie."

They stepped out briskly. It was warm but not too warm yet. Once they had left the Platz behind them, they broke up into knots and clusters of three or four and strolled along, talking gaily.

"Are we going up by the stream?" Jack asked Miss Ferrars who was near.

"No; we're turning up the road that leads to the motor-traffic bridge. It's shorter that way and the sooner we reach our destination, the better. It's going to be baking hot day."

Gillie made a face. "I don't exactly love that way," she said.

"Not? But – oh, of course! I'd forgotten that business when you folk were lost in those woods.[1] Well, Gillie, I promise not to lose you this time," Miss Ferrars said solemnly, but with a wicked twinkle. "Anyhow, it won't be dark until long after we get back."

"What was all that in aid of?" Jane asked José in an undertone.

José giggled. "Jack and her gang lost themselves up there last Christmas term. They had a ghastly time of it. Mary Candlish cut her foot badly and they had to carry her most of the way. It was pitch dark and half the mistresses and all the prefects were out hunting for them. In fact," José wound up airily, "a good time was had by all!"

Jane broke into a peal of laughter. "It sounds like it! Oh, my dear, what a ghastly set-out! I'd hate to be lost in the woods myself!"

"Turn, you people!" came Miss Wilmot's voice. "Up to the bridge and then on past it. We're going to camp in that open space where the great boulder is."

The girls turned up the road cut through the pines which led to a stout stone bridge, built to carry all heavy

[1] *The Feud in the Chalet School.*

motor traffic to and from the Platz. Jane had not seen it before and she exclaimed at the height of the arch.

"Why *is* it so raised?" she exclaimed. "And what a distance it begins along the road!"

"Floods!" José said, hanging over the parapet to stare down at the trickle of water meandering round the pebbles on its bed.

"*Floods!* But darling! Not that tiny brook, surely!"

"You don't know what our thunderstorms can be like!" Dilys grinned, coming up in time to overhear. "Does she, folk?"

"It's true all right," José said. "You just ask Len Maynard. She's *experienced* it!"

"What's that?" Len's quick ears had caught her own name.

José explained and Len laughed. "It's certainly true. I don't think I was ever so scared in my life as when we had to wade across a young pond with the current from the stream pelting down at such a rate I thought I was going to be taken off my feet any moment!"[1]

"Tell – tell!" Jane begged.

"OK, but come back to the path. We've got to go on up." She led them off the bridge and, as they climbed up the steepening path, she told the story of that truly alarming experience.

"How too, too ghastly!" Jane exclaimed when it finished. Her grey eyes were wide. With her vivid imagination she could both see and feel that torrent for the moment.

"It was! However, it's not likely to happen again. They've deepened the edge of the stream and built up the banks – see! And further up, they've cut channels to

[1] *The Chalet School and Richenda.*

carry off surplus water. And by the same token, here *is* one of those channels!" Len pointed to a plank bridge set across a deep ditch.

The girls skipped across, then they turned to the left and at last reached the place for their camp, a clearing among the pines, in the middle of which stood an enormous boulder, relic of a much earlier flood.

"Here at last!" Len said, with a sigh of relief. "Squat, people! I'm sure it's time for elevenses. My inside clock says so, anyhow!"

Amidst peals of laughter, they squatted. The picnic had begun.

CHAPTER 13

Tree'd!

"Hurry up and settle down!" Nancy Wilmot commanded when the last of her charges arrived at the boulder. "I don't know about you people, but I want my elevenses. This side of the rock please, Kitty! Or else keep your hat on!"

Kitty hurriedly shuffled along to the side where the shadow of the rock shielded them from the worst of the sun's rays. It was well after 10.00 hours now and he was getting down to his job with much enthusiasm. The big basket carried between Barbara and Val yielded up its treasure and they sat round, drinking Karen's delicious iced lemonade and munching her famous lemon biscuits. After the long pull up the mountain path they were glad of a short rest and, for a while, even the chatter was sparse. Then restless Jack proposed a game of hide-and-seek, with the boulder for Home.

"It'll be too hot to play later," she argued. "Let's have a crack at it now."

Miss Wilmot laughed. "Oh, very well; but on one condition. After we've had our midday meal, you all stay quiet for at least an hour. Agreed?"

They all agreed with enthusiasm. Len and Ruey were chosen for seekers and the rest, including the mistresses, scattered among the trees while the two seniors religiously shut their eyes and began counting aloud.

Jack scrambled as noiselessly as she could up the far side of the rock – and later, wished she hadn't. It was hot

130

already and lying there as flat as she could, she felt the sun beating down on her back. Wanda crawled into a nook at one side. José, clutching Jane's hand, scuttled off to the stream, where they clambered down the bank to hide themselves under the shadow of a big thornbush which grew there. The rest sought the woods.

"Ninety-nine – a hundred!" came Len's voice in a warning shriek. "We're coming!" There was a moment's silence than she shouted again. "Jack Lambert! Come down! You're on top of the rock!"

Jack's crimson face peered over the edge. "How *did* you know?"

"Heard someone climbing up," returned lynx-eared Len. "You come down! Catch her, Ruey!"

Jack scrambled down and began to fan herself with her hat. "Phew! It's hot up there!"

A yell from Ruey, who had been scouting round the rock, announced that Wanda had been caught, and then the seekers set off to the trees. One by one the hiders were discovered, till finally only Jane and José were left.

They took some finding, but at last Ruey spotted a fold of José's pink gingham and with a yell of: "José and Jane! Come *out!* You're caught!" She dived for Home, easily beating them.

"How did you know Jane was there too?" José demanded.

"Because you two seem to hunt in couples," Ruey responded. "Jack and Wanda, it's your turn to seek. Come on, everyone!"

Once more they scattered but, warned by Ruey's word, bosom friends parted and hid by themselves after that.

"Ruey," José remarked as she left Jane, "knows a lot too much!"

Presently, the seekers were Arda Peik and Jane herself.

131

Much to their delight, Arda caught Miss Wilmot and Jane unearthed Margot Maynard almost at once. Some of the others took a little finding, however. Jack was the last and no one could see her anywhere. Time was passing and already Kathy Ferrars had suggested to her colleague that they should have a meal after this round and then rest. When no Jack turned up, she and Nancy set the girls to calling, but no answer came.

"Oh, my only Aunt Sempronia!" Margot exclaimed. "Let's hope she hasn't done something mad and hurt herself. We'd better all look. She might have banged her head somehow and knocked herself out."

"*Need* you make such horrible suggestions?" Miss Wilmot demanded. "All the same, we'd better all join in. Off you go, girls! Miss Ferrars, you go along the stream, will you, and I'll walk down through those trees there. Don't go far, any of you, and yell if you get into difficulties or find Jack in one. Time yourselves. Ten minutes and then report back here."

They set off, everyone choosing a different direction, though they were all within calling distance of each other. They hunted industriously, but not a sign of Jack could they find. Len, remembering her first effort, climbed up the boulder but she was not there. Kitty Anderson crawled as far under it as she could, but no Jack was curled up in any nook or cranny. Every tree and bush was examined and still no Jack!

"Where on earth can she be?" Miss Ferrars exclaimed when the ten minutes had ended and most of them were standing round the boulder. "We gave you your bounds while we had elevenses and I don't imagine she would exceed them."

"One moment!" Miss Wilmot interrupted her. "Where's Jane Carew? *She* seems to be missing now."

She scanned the big group of girls, but nowhere were Jane's green frock and long fair plaits to be seen.

"P'raps Jane's found Jack and is staying to help her along," Gillies suggested. "Jack might have given her ankle a twist or something."

"That's an idea!" Len exclaimed. "Shall we have another look?"

"Yes – at least you three Maynards, Ruey and I will," Miss Wilmot said. "The rest of you be setting out our meal. Miss Ferrars!" To her friend she said in an aside, "If we aren't back in about twenty minutes time, start them on their eats. But I expect we'll find that pair before then." She went off once more with her chosen team, feeling worried, however lightly she might have treated it before the girls.

Meanwhile Jane, going along a narrow path, little more than a timber-run, which wound through the pines and towards the next mountain-shelf, was having an adventure all her own. She had reached the bounds given them in that direction and was about to turn back to report failure when directly overhead she heard a queer noise, half gulp, half croak. She looked up, but the trees were large and heavy with their summer pine-needles and she could see nothing.

"Jack! Is that you?" she called; and the same sound came again.

"Where are you? – Wait! I'm going back a little. I can't see a thing from here!" And Jane retreated a little way down the path and stared up again at the thickly-needled giant which was also supporting another as large as itself. One of the winter storms must have partly uprooted it and it had fallen against the trunk of the first one. Between the two, it was not easy to see much but green; but as Jane sidled round it a little, she caught a glimpse of yellow and

133

gave a yell of triumph. Jack was there all right; but why did she not come down?

Jane stepped back once more and then things were plain to her. There, astride a bough not far from the top of the first tree, was Jack. She was doubled up in an odd position and while she clung to her bough with one hand, she seemed to be wrenching at the back of her frock with the other.

"Jack!" Jane cried. "Oh, my dear, what *are* you doing? We've looked everywhere for you! Do come down as fast as you can!"

Jack's face was mainly hidden by small branches and for some reason, she appeared to find it hard to talk. "Don't be an ass!" came to Jane in muffled tones. "I'm caught! I'm half-strangled, what's more! Some beastly twig has caught in the neck of my frock and it's twisted tight and I can't get it out!"

The bough she was straddling gave a loud creak as she wrenched fiercely again. Jane eyed it anxiously.

"Do keep as still as you can!" she called. "I rather think that branch is feeling your weight and if – Hi!" as it groaned again, "keep still, Jack, and try to hang on to another branch if you possibly can. I'm coming up to undo you, but do keep still or you may have a nasty fall!"

Jack had no idea who had come to her assistance. She could see nothing for the pine-needles and, to tell the truth, plucky girl as she was, she was rapidly reaching a state of panic. She guessed as well as Jane what might happen to her bough, and her mind was too full of that for her to bother about anything else.

"OK!" she got out. "But do be quick!"

Without much ado, Jane sprang as high as she could, caught hold of a low-growing branch and heaved herself up till she could reach a hand to a higher one. She was as agile as a monkey, but even so, reaching Jack was no easy matter. She had to go carefully, for some of the boughs were slender ones and she dared not trust her weight on them. The leaning pine added to the difficulties, for some of its branches were thrust through those of the first one, complicating matters. Jane went as fast as she could, for continued creaks and groans warned her that Jack's bough was not going to stand the strain much longer, and though Jack *might* be able to save herself from going completely headlong, she would certainly be hurt in some way. She was a long way up and a fall from that height could mean serious damage.

To Jack, wondering how much longer the bough and she could hold out, it seemed a century before she caught a glimpse of a flutter of green and white and knew that her rescuer was somewhere near. She had contrived to grip a higher branch with one hand, but it was slender and she could reach nothing else that looked like being of the slightest use.

Slowly, steadily, the green and white flutter came nearer. Then it stopped. There was an exclamation followed by silence. A loud "Ow-w!" reached her. Then an arm was pushed through the nearby branches and a hand fumbled for her.

"OK," Jack said shakily. "You're nearly there. Do be careful, though! This beastly bough is giving. It'll go any moment so keep clear of it. Can you see where I'm hooked? Haul me free – tear my frock: that'll do it. I can manage for myself, then."

"Right!" The voice was muffled, for Jane's face was buried in pine-needles and she had a mouthful to contend with. Somehow, she had to get across the trunk of the fallen tree at this point and it wasn't going to be easy.

She shifted one scratched leg and got it across. Clinging

to a sturdy bough just above her head, she contrived to bring the other over and then, at the cost of a bump over one eye, she found herself immediately behind Jack.

She saw at a glance what had happened. The back of the neck of the prisoner's frock had caught on a short stump. Somehow – probably through her own gyrations – it had got twisted tightly, preventing her from calling loudly and half-choking her. Her head was forced sideways under another branch to which she was clinging with one hand while the other held on to the one she straddled. Jane glanced down and saw that it was tearing away from the trunk. Also, which alarmed her even more, it seemed to be half-dead, for the needles were turning brown. No wonder it was giving under Jack's weight!

Jane straightened up, set her teeth and tried to drag the frock clear. It was so twisted, she found it impossible. Moving carefully, she managed to stand up, lean against the sturdy trunk of the tree and then, greatly daring and gripping with the feet from which she had already kicked off her sandals, she took both hands to the task.

It was a mercy that it was one of last summer's frocks and that Jack's frocks were frequently subjected to bad treatment. New material would have resisted anything Jane could do. But she had gripped it at a weak place in the hem, and it gave after as hefty a tug as she could manage. It was better then. Jane yanked and it tore right up. Jack released the hand on her big bough, pulled as hard as she could on her belt which had needed a stitch or two, anyhow; the final threads holding the buckle snapped and the belt fell so that Jane was able to rip the remainder right up to the neck. Another heave and the neck gave. Jack, able to breathe freely at last, sighed deeply.

"Get your arms out!" Jane gasped. "That bough's going!"

Jack snatched her arms out and Jane grabbed her shoulder just as the bough, with a horrible splintering noise, tore clean away from the parent trunk and crashed through its mates, down to the ground. The maltreated frock followed it a yard or two then was caught on a lower bough just as Jack, knowing that the other branch to which she was clinging was likely to go shortly, kicked out wildly and got one foot into a crotch a little lower down.

Jane clung to her shoulder to steady her, at the same time crouching down on her knees to get a better purchase. To Jack it felt as if her shoulder was being wrenched out, but she set her teeth, felt with her free hand for the bough below, got it, and then said, "L-let me go a m-minute! I'm OK!"

Jane shook her head – or tried to. One of her pigtails had caught now. She hauled it free, lowered herself carefully, never once losing her grip on Jack, and then contrived to get an arm round Jack's waist and gripped the top of that young woman's knickers with her fingers.

More, they could not do. Jane yelled as loudly as she could. Jack's throat was still too dry for her to do more than croak. It was a blessing for them that Miss Wilmot, hunting frantically for them, was only a few yards away and heard Jane's shrieks. She came at top speed to where the fallen bough lay across the path. Another ear-splitting yell from above made her look up. What she saw told her the main points of the story.

"Jane – Jack!" she called. "Are you safe for the moment?"

The branches were wildly agitated and Jane's face,

white, streaked with dirt and with loose hair hanging over it, peered down at her.

"We can't get further," she said simply.

"All right. Keep quite still as long as those boughs are steady. I'll shout for help and we'll have you down in a jiffy! I can't manage alone." And Nancy raised her voice and produced a bellow she had not known she could accomplish.

It reached Len Maynard and Betty Landon, both of whom came tearing up from opposite directions. They wasted no time in chatter. They had seen what was wrong as they came and, without more ado, Len went up the tree like a lamplighter, Betty not far behind her.

"Careful, girls!" Miss Wilmot said sharply. "Not too high, either of you! That's right, Len; move Jack's foot to that next bough. Betty, help Jane. Let go of Jack, Jane! Len has her safely now."

It was only a few seconds before first Jack and then Jane was safely on the path, each with the much-needed arm of a Senior flung round her to steady her. Both were white from strain and terror, for those last few moments had seemed like years; but, apart from scratches, grazes and bumps, neither was badly hurt, though Jack, minus her frock and with her knickers torn down one leg was a sight to behold. Jane's frock was filthy, but it was whole. She had lost both hair-ribbons and her plaits had come undone and were streaming round her. Both girls were further adorned with pine-needles and bits of bark. As for their hands and legs and faces, both looked as if they had been playing in a coal-cellar.

"First things first!" Nancy Wilmot reminded herself grimly. Aloud, she said, "Can you two walk? You can? Then come along!"

They struggled back to camp. Halfway there, they were

met by Margot, Con, Alicia Leonard and Miss Ferrars, who had heard Miss Wilmot's ringing call of "Found safely!" and the elder girls insisted on chairing the two victims the rest of the way.

Arrived at the clearing, they were carefully lowered to their feet when Jack disgraced herself in her own eyes by keeling over in a faint. Jane did keep her feet, but she was thankful to sit down. She was shaking from head to foot and her legs felt like sticks of boiled macaroni.

The two mistresses coped instantly. They sent all the girls but Len and Alicia to start their meal while Miss Ferrars produced the first-aid case, doctored Jack with a dose of sal volatile – her faintness had lasted very briefly – and then attended to the wounds of both with iodine and Bandaid. After that, cups of hot coffee revived them considerably and they were able to make a fair meal. But once that was over, the question arose of what to do about their clothes. Water from the brook had cleaned their faces; someone had produced a comb and Jane's hair was once more in its plaits, though they had to be tied with some knitting wool from Betty's bag. But Jane's frock was a mess and Jack was half-naked.

Len solved the problem. "I'll fly home – I know a short-cut – and get some things for them," she said. "There are heaps of our outgrown things packed away till Felicity grows to them. We can rig them out all right. It's no use going to School for their own, is it? Isn't it closed for the day?"

"Yes, even Karen and Co have gone off for a picnic on their own," Miss Ferrars said. "That's a good idea, Len; but take Con or Margot with you."

"Yes indeed!" Miss Wilmot fully agreed with this. "Go carefully, you two. They can take a nap while you're gone and they won't hurt in this hot weather. But for pity's sake, no more accidents! I feel weak with this latest affair as it is."

It was arranged. Everyone was ordered to take a rest and Jane and Jack were settled in the most comfortable place of all. Len and Con set off for Freudesheim, whence they returned laden with frocks, underclothes, sandals and a very full sponge-bag and towels. Len had even remembered ribbons for Jane's pigtails. By the time she was decently clean and clad, Jane felt much more like herself after her peaceful nap. Jack, on the other hand, had not slept at all. She had too much to think about! It was all very well and she was grateful to Jane for coming to the rescue, but it did make a mess of things. For how could she possibly go on hating Jane now; and, being Jack, how could she suddenly turn round and do the other thing.

CHAPTER 14

Joey's Inspiration

JANE and Jack heard very little then about their adventure. For one thing, the authorities thought the less said the better: Matey dosed them both before they went to bed and, in consequence, they had a good night's sleep and woke up feeling themselves again: only their honourable scars remained to remind anyone of what had occurred. For another, tree-climbing was not forbidden at the school so no rules had been broken.

"We'll leave it to Matey," the Head decided when she had heard the whole tale. "She'll have plenty to say to them about their clothes. But I will warn the whole school about testing branches before they climb them unless they want the game to be banned altogether."

It was left at that and, in any case, Saturday night saw the revival of Mrs Jarley's Waxworks and, by the time it was over, the entire audience had nearly laughed themselves into stitches and even Jane and Jack had forgotten the previous day's experience.

On the Sunday they spent the day as usual with church-going, quiet rambles and, in the evening, sitting about the garden with books, and reading or gossiping. Monday was different.

"It's raining – it's simply pouring down!" said Joey Maynard as she sat up in bed and stared out of the nearest lattice. "What *will* they do with the entire school on their hands? I can fill in the evening all right!" she giggled at

141

the thought. "But there's the whole day first. Let me think!"

The result of her cogitations was that when she was dressed and downstairs, she spent a short time on the telephone, reducing both herself and Miss Annersley to fits of laughter.

"Tell the girls *I'm* arranging this evening," she directed her friend, "but don't tell them *how*. They'll be well occupied trying to guess!"

Miss Annersley duly made the announcement after Prayers and Joey proved herself right. The school spent quite a lot of time trying to guess just what was in store for them. They had been told to spend the morning in their common rooms, for the prefects were hurriedly getting up Progressive Games to fill in the afternoon and required Hall to arrange it. Halfway through the morning, Jane and Adrienne, going to the library to change their books, ran into Mrs Maynard in the entrance hall. She gave an exclamation at sight of Jane's face.

"My dear girl! You look as if you'd taken on your weight in wild cats and got the worst of it! Was all this your tree-climbing effort?"

Jane grinned. "But darling, you've no idea how those pine-needles prickled! I'll never climb another pine if I can help it. And you ought to see Jack's face! Mine has nothing on hers!"

"Heaven help her! It's just as well neither of your families can see what you look like at that rate. That's a handsome lump over your left eye, Jane. *That* wasn't done by pine-needles!"

"No – a ghastly bough that I banged against. Margot *told* me I looked like a prize-fighter when she saw me this morning. My head ached all yesterday afternoon and evening, but it's all right today. I'm all ready to enjoy what you've planned for us. What is it? Do give us just the *teeniest* hint!"

"Not the merest sniff of a hint!" Joey said firmly. "I'm going. See you all tonight!" And she shot off in the direction of the Head's annexe leaving them unsatisfied, but pleasingly thrilled all the same.

Progressive Games kept them busy all the afternoon. The prefects had racked their brains for new ideas and in addition to the usual run, the girls found themselves cutting out silhouettes; picking up butter-beans with their toes and depositing them in basins; trying to push peas up a ramp made with a ruler, using an orange-stick for pusher; and making sevenfold plaits of long strands of variously-coloured wools. As a final effort, small boxes crammed with a mixture of peas, haricot beans, lentils, rice, silver cachous and beads had to be sorted out into their component parts and, with a bare ten minutes at their disposal, the girls did not find that easy. Prizes were awarded – mainly sweets from the hostesses' tuck boxes – at the end of the afternoon and, as Prudence Dawbarn observed, a good time was had by all.

Meanwhile the Staff had been called to Joey's assistance and spent their time quite agreeably making up bundles of clothes of every kind. Envelopes, containing slips which Rosalie Dene spent most of her morning typing, were tied in with them and they were piled up handily at the back of the daïs in Hall, together with some of the carrying-trays used during packing and unpacking. Karen and her minions also spent a busy time, turning out a supper which would rejoice the heart of anyone but a confirmed dyspeptic. In short, everyone was busy and everyone was happy.

"Do *we* join in this?" Nancy Wilmot demanded halfway

through the afternoon, as she tossed a bundle to Jo who was labelling them.

"We do – Daisy and me into the bargain."

Daisy Rosomon giggled. "It's not completely original, but it has original ideas to it. I wouldn't miss it for something!"

"When are they to dress?" Ruth Derwent asked.

"After they've all got their bundles."

"We'll have a riot on our hands!" Sharley Andrews prophesied.

"Not us! Hilda will look at them with her famous 'Girls-I'm-shocked-at-you!' expression and that'll settle them. I know what it did to *me* when I was their age!" Joey said, giggling like one of her own daughters. "How many more to do, someone? We'll have earned our Kaffee und Kuchen when we get it!"

A message was sent to the Speisesaal to the effect that no one was to change but everyone was to make herself tidy before coming down to Hall. They were to sit down on the first seat available and wait until they were told what to do.

"Oh, what *can* it be?" Jane wondered excitedly.

"Goodness knows! With Auntie Jo in charge it may be anything!" José said with a gurgle. "She can think of the maddest things!"

They wasted little time after that. By 17.30 hours everyone was seated in Hall, where some of the mistresses were already waiting to take charge. Only the Kindergarten and Forms IIA and B were missing. They were in the gymnasium, playing games, with four of the staff to look after them; later, they would be relieved by four more; others would take *their* turns later still. No one wanted to miss all of Joey's latest inspiration.

As the chime for the half-hour rang out, the Head

arrived, escorted by all the other mistresses not already employed. Miss Derwent and Miss Yolland pulled back the curtains which had hidden the trays already loaded with bundles and then, two by two, the mistresses seized them and proceeded to give out the bundles. When the last had been delivered, Joey mounted the daïs, clutching her own share.

"Now!" she said with a complacent grin. "In your envelopes, you will find slips bearing the names of famous people – some real ones, others from books. You are to dress up as your character and for the rest of the time before Abendessen you are to try to resemble that character as far as you can in speech and manner." Here she paused, for gasps were going round. Then she resumed sweetly. "You are to tell no one who you are, and you are to write down the names of as many as you can guess – name of character and name of person. There are sheets of paper and pencils for you on that table. If you want more paper, you may have it. There are prizes for the best lists and a special prize for whoever, in the considered opinions of Miss Annersley, Miss Derwent, Miss Charlesworth, Miss Yolland and myself, best represents her character. Please wait till I get back to my seat. I'm in this as well as you!" She bounded off the daïs and ran to her seat amid loud applause. The Head waited till she was seated. Then she grabbed up her own bundle from beside her chair and said, "Begin! Open your envelopes and find out who you are!"

A chorus of exclamations, laughter and groans followed. Then Joey called, "Go to your form rooms and change. You have ten minutes from – NOW!"

They were up and off and it was as well that the two sets of double doors at either end of Hall were wide. As it was, the place was cleared in short order, the staff racing off to the library which had been set apart for them. Ten minutes were none too long to change and decide how your character would talk and behave.

Jane, on opening her slip, had discovered that she was Queen Victoria as a little girl, and groaned, for she knew very little about that famous Queen and nothing at all about her girlhood.

"Oh, how terrible!" she exclaimed. "I've not the least idea – "

"Scrub it!" Jack, who was nearest her, ordered. "You'll be giving it away next minute, fathead!"

"So I shall! Oh, darling, how sweet of you to remind me!" Jane cried.

"Huh!" Jack grunted. She still could not like Jane, though it made her feel an ungrateful pig whenever she thought of it; but, having got off on the wrong foot with the new girl, Jack, being Jack, found it hard to change. She turned her back on Jane and slipped off her frock before pulling on the pair of ragged trousers and shirt she found to help her represent Dr Barnardo's earliest waif and stray.

Combs, brushes, pins of every kind, and mirrors had been provided in each room. Certain of the bundles contained wigs from the acting cupboards. Ten minutes was short measure to attend to all this, and they had to scurry. Jane, with a vague recollection of pictures she had seen, brushed out her hair, divided it into strands which she back-combed and then rolled into curls to be pinned as securely as she could manage round her head so that she had ringlets. Jack merely ran her fingers through her cropped black locks till they stood on end. As a final attempt at realism, she wiped her hands round the cupboard floor and gave her face a liberal coating of dust.

The bell rang to recall them to Hall and it was a very

motley gathering that assembled there finally. An obvious Napoleon Bonaparte rubbed shoulders with a lady who later transpired to be Mrs Malaprop. The Waif and Stray was seated next to Alice in Wonderland. Queen Victoria as a child found herself between a Red Indian, whom she later put down as Hiawatha, and a gentleman in Roman toga with crown of laurel leaves and harp – and only three people guessed him to be Nero. The rest mostly pitched on Julius Caesar or, a select few, Horace.

Jane had little idea how the good queen would have talked and behaved. Certainly she would use no slang, nor was she likely to say "prithee' or "eftsoons". She finally compromised on being very stately and dignified and her language was primmest of the prim.

Miss Andrews, who represented the queen in her later years and wore a small crown and veil with broad blue sash slung across one shoulder, was curt in manner and almost none of the younger girls guessed her. But an unguarded, "We are *not* amused!" spoken with a giggle hitched fore and aft, in reply to some banter on her manner from Joey, got up as the tallest of English kings, Edward III, gave her away to all those Seniors within hearing.

It was tremendous fun and Hall rang with their laughter. It was even funnier when Miss Annersley finally called a halt to their guessing. She told them all to sit and correct their papers while the various people would be called into the middle of Hall in turn to announce who they represented.

Joey, the first to be called, set the example for this. Stalking to her place, she bowed deeply and stated with a most unkingly grin, "I'm Lanky Ned, alias Edward III of England." She got roars of laughter as well as cheers and clapping, and had fitted the poor king with a sobriquet he never lost among that generation of Chalet girls.

Jane, some ten personages later, walked with great dignity to the spot, swept a curtsy to all four sides and said, "I am the Princess Victoria of England." She curtsied again and returned to her chair with the same dignity.

"One thing she has in common with the great Victoria," Joey murmured to the Head who was sitting next her.

"You mean grace of movement?"

"That, of course; and also a clear, silvery voice. But she has looks, too, has our Jane and that, to judge by all the portraits I've ever seen, Victoria never had. How could she, poor soul, with her rabbity mouth? A pity they didn't have straightening bands for children's teeth in those days, but I suppose no one ever though of it then."

Miss Annersley laughed and went on with her work, for time was flying and supper was awaiting them. She herself as Boudicca, the famous warrior queen, came last. Then they had to count up their guesses. Considering the number and variety of the characters, no one did very brilliantly. Anna Hoffman of IVA claimed sixty-one and Eloïse Dafflon and Len Maynard tied with fifty-seven. None of the others had achieved more than forty and Jack came bottom with only seven! Jane, much to her delight, headed Upper IVB with thirty-seven correct guesses. The prizes, presented by Joey, were copies of her own books. The Seniors and Staff received historical novels and the younger girls school or adventure stories. Jack won the prize for impersonating a street urchin successfully. She deserved it, for she had turned somersaults and cartwheels, walked on her hands, whistled shrilly and exruciatingly until stopped firmly by Miss Derwent, and relapsed into broad Cheshire when anyone addressed her. Lizette Falence was judged best among the Seniors with her representation of the Abbé Liszt. To her, Joey gave a delightful string of Venetian beads, but when it came to Jack's turn, she put aside the dainty brooch she had chosen for the purpose and asked what Jack would like.

"A book about cars," Jack said instantly – "all about how they were invented and the different makes and famous drivers and things like that."

"Right, but you'll have to wait for it. Dr Rosomon is going to England on business next week and he'll get it for you," Joey said amiably.

"Smashing!" ejaculated Jack, using a strictly forbidden word. But for once, she got away with it. The gong sounded and they went in to Abendessen where Karen's contribution received its full meed of praise.

She had provided chicken salad, creams and jellies in quantity, meringues smothered in whipped cream, bowls of fruit floating in amber or ruby syrup, a variety of Swiss pastries and, as a wind-up, ices of five kinds – vanilla, strawberry, coffee, lemon, and pistachio. Chilled fruit drinks gleamed in glass pitchers and later, for those who liked it, there came black coffee in tiny cups.

"Hope you've got gallons of castor oil, Matey," Jo remarked to that lady as she finished her third ice. "You'll need it!"

"No; but I've any amount of syrup of figs," Matey retorted. "I'll give you a dose before you go home or *you'll* be needing it tomorrow. You're as bad as any schoolgirl, Joey!"

"Well, you may not know it, but for tonight, I *am* a schoolgirl," Joey informed her. "I'll risk it, thank you! I know your doses of old and I'd rather be excused!"

She wound up with a wicked chuckle and Matey, baffled for once, merely looked at her witheringly before she turned away to regard with horror Jack Lambert draining her fifth glass of fruit drink after a gargantuan meal in which she had sampled everything once.

"I'm in for a restless night!" the school tyrant decided, tasting her coffee. Then she laughed. It was unlikely to hurt the girls for once.

CHAPTER 15

Janice Creates a Sensation

TUESDAY proved a fine day so the girls spent it out of doors and made the most of it. The serious half of the term was just on them, what with the public examinations, the regatta they were hoping to hold this year, their annual Sale, and Sports Day. For some of the Seniors, the end of term would mean goodbye to school and the beginning of their careers. Others would go to St Mildred's for a final year at the finishing branch. This mainly affected members of VIA and B though Tina Harms and Odette Mercier of VA were also leaving. Tina's people were going to join a relative on his ranch in America and Odette's mother, who had been a long time at the Sanatorium but was now much better, was to take an ocean voyage to seal her recovery and Odette was going with her. Mme Mercier would be at sea for some months and she refused to be parted so long from her only child, especially as Odette was fatherless, which made them cling even more closely together.

The girls said goodbye to all the half-term fun with regret and returned to their usual work and play, and by the end of the week were well into harness. Jane had settled in thoroughly and was a regular Chalet School girl now. She was working hard and had the hope that by the end of term, apart from geometry, which remained her bugbear, she would be able to work with her own form in all subjects. Latin, said Miss Derwent, she had simply absorbed. Her grammar was still weak, but she would soon make that up. Miss Wilmot and Miss Ferrars agreed that she could very well work with Upper IVв in both algebra and arithmetic. This left geometry and Miss Ferrars offered to surrender a precious free half-hour to give her more extra coaching.

"It's very good of her," Jane told José when she had heard this. "In fact, it's too, *too* kind; but I doubt if even that will make much difference. I haven't *got* a geometrical brain and no amount of coaching will ever give me one. I do wish I needn't do it!"

"Well, you aren't taking science, so it'll have to be maths," José pointed out. "Hard luck, Jane!"

Jane thought it very hard luck indeed. She said nothing about it in her letters to Australia, but she had fully determined that once she was there she would try to coax her parents into saying that she need not take it. After all, you didn't need geometry for an acting career and that, she had made up her mind, was her future job.

Apart from that, she had only one complaint to make. She had seen little or nothing of Switzerland, except their immediate surroundings.

"I do wish we could have *one* real expedition like those you've talked about," she said one evening when a dozen of them were resting after a severe tennis practice.

"Don't you wish you may get it!" Jack remarked. She had been undergoing a strenuous time at the nets and had come to join the others for the time left before Abendessen. "When we aren't even allowed to go down to the lake you bet they won't give us a sniff of an expedition. I don't see why not myself. We haven't had a solitary case up here and we've all been vaccinated. We ought to be safe enough."

"Oh, but Jack, you can't be *sure*," Jane said earnestly.

"How do *you* know?" Jack demanded. "You aren't a doctor."

"No; but I have heard of it happening. It would be ghastly if we did get it here. What would happen to our regatta and all the rest you've told me of?"

The bell recalling them to tidy for their meal pealed out and they had to leave the question. Jane ran off with José, and Jack, waiting until the others had gone on ahead, followed them, a frown knitting her brow.

She was in a real quandary. She felt that she ought to like Jane Carew who had, as she had been informed by more than one of the Seniors, risked her own life to get her down from that tree; but she couldn't.

"I don't see why," Jack mused as she sauntered along. "She's not bad as girls go. She's getting better over the way she talks and she doesn't fly at people as she used to. She's not like me, of course. In fact, I should think she's the exact opposite. Perhaps that's why. Oh, I do feel so muddled about it!"

"Hurry up, Jack, or you will be late," observed Lizette behind her. "Come! Make haste!"

Jack hurried herself a little and contrived to slide into her place in time, but she was very silent throughout the meal. Then, after Prayers, the Head threw a bombshell into their midst.

"I'm very sorry, girls," she said, "but I'm afraid we must give up the idea of our regatta, for this term at any rate. There are a little more than five weeks left and ten days of that time is taken up by the exams. Smallpox is still about and until it ends, we dare not let you run any risks. As soon as the doctors tell us it is safe, you shall go down as usual; but I don't see how we can possibly hope to work the regatta in in the time."

It was a blow to more than one, Jack among them. She

gave up worrying about her private problems to join in the general outcry, once they were free to voice their opinions aloud; and before the said problems had time to come uppermost again, Janice Chester provided the school with a sensation it would have been glad to be spared.

On the Tuesday after half-term week, Janice was unaccountably quiet, even for her. Her special chums, Ailie Russell and Judy Willoughby, noticed that she ate much less than usual, but when they commented on it, she snapped at them and told them to mind their own business in no uncertain tones.

"Toothache, perhaps," said Ailie when they had left her with some dignity.

"In that case, Matey will find out and it means the dentist." Judy shivered realistically. "Poor old Jan! If it's that, I don't wonder she snapped!"

"Better leave her alone," Ailie said sagely. "You *don't* want people fussing round when you've got toothache."

They left it at that and Janice who was really feeling miserable and rather sick, was left to herself for the rest of the day.

On the Wednesday morning, she reluctantly presented herself to Matey to own that she had a nasty headache and "felt queer".

"Sick?" Matey asked, getting out her thermometer.

"A little. It's more being achey and hotty-cold," Janice confessed.

"I see." Matey popped the thermometer into her mouth. "Now stop talking and keep that under your tongue."

When she removed the thermometer and looked at it, she nodded. "H'm! A couple of days in San for you, my child! You're up a point or two. Come along! I'll take you to Nurse. No; never mind your night things. We'll see about those later." And she marched Janice off and handed her over to Nurse.

Janice went to bed; Dr Maynard was rung up; and everyone in authority redoubled their vigilance.

When the doctor arrived later, he turned out to be a new-comer to the Sanatorium, a young man not long out of his training. He brought a note from Jack Maynard for the Head.

"Dear Hilda," Jack had written, "Sorry I can't come myself, but the San has to be my first consideration as you know, and with the number of serious cases we have at the moment, I daren't run any risks. I'm sending Gordon along. It's probably only the aftermath of half-term, but he'll report to me after he's seen Janice. Yours in a rush, Jack.

P.S. Don't panic. The thing seems to be dying out definitely now. No fresh cases reported for five days."

Dr Gordon examined his patient thoroughly, but so far was unable to say what the trouble was. Janice was running a temperature and was very wretched and unwell, but there was nothing really positive – yet.

That came next day when a couple of nasty spots appeared on her chin. There was another in her hair and the temperature had risen rather alarmingly. He shook his head, but they could only follow the prescribed treatment.

"*Is* it smallpox?" Miss Annersley asked anxiously when he came to report.

"I still can't say certainly, but it looks rather like it. I hoped it was only going to be an extra bad case of chicken-pox, but those aren't chickenpox spots. I'll come along again later in the day. Meantime, she's having everything we can do for her and she's been vaccinated lately, so it shouldn't be a bad case if it *is* that."

155

"And I honestly don't see what more we can do," a worried Miss Annersley told Joey when that young woman rang her up during the morning. "Janice has a high temperature and there are those spots. I ought to let the Chesters know, but Anne sailed for the South Seas last week for that year with Elizabeth she's been talking about, so she may be anywhere now. And when she wrote last week, she said that Peter was running the practice single-handed as his partner had a smash-up with his motor-cycle and was in hospital with compound fracture of the leg and locums weren't to be had for love or money."

"Heavens! What a mess!" Joey said.

"I wish we could call in one of the older doctors. Young Gordon is a very nice lad, but he hasn't had the experience of the others."

"You can't do that, my dear. It wouldn't be etiquette! Look here! You cable Peter Chester and see what *he* says. He'll manage somehow; and he's the kid's father and has every right to visit her if he can."

The cable was sent at once. Dr Chester's reply told them that he was flying across from Guernsey that night. An old hospital friend had turned up unexpectedly and had agreed to take over the practice for the time being. The Head told Dr Gordon when he came for his second visit, by which time Janice was nearly covered with spots.

"I'm thankful!" he said. "I just *can't* say if it's smallpox or not. Those spots look like it, but other symptoms don't. I wish one of the other men could come along, but apart from any danger of taking infection to the Sanatorium, we're full up – some very bad cases, too – and everyone's just about run off their feet!"

Dr Chester arrived early next morning and demanded to be taken to see his daughter at once. Janice had had a better night. She had had an hour or two of quiet sleep and the temperature had definitely dropped, Nurse reported. She was awake when he arrived and she managed a shadowy smile as he bent over her.

"Daddy!" she murmured. "How nice!"

"Just a flying visit! Now, old lady, let's have a look at you."

He finished his examination, by which time Janice had drowsed off again.

"Well?" Nurse asked anxiously.

He grinned. "Not smallpox, I think. I'll see her again, but it's not that. What's she having in the way of nourishment?"

They went into a medical huddle, but he refused to say more until a second visit which he paid her at about ten o'clock. Dr Gordon had arrived and the two doctors went upstairs together. Nurse met them with a smile.

"Definite improvement," she said. "The temp's still dropping a little and she asked for milk and drank all I gave her. She had a good nap and now she's awake."

This time, Dr Chester gave her a thorough examination, the younger man watching him anxiously. When at last he stood up, he patted the patient's shoulder.

"*You'll* be all right before long," he told her. "Do exactly as Nurse says and unless you want to be marked, *don't* try to scratch."

Janice grinned at him weakly. "They itch like stink!" she murmured.

"I daresay! That won't last long if you leave them alone." He gave her a smile and turned to collect Dr Gordon and Nurse with a look. In the outer room, the Head was waiting for them.

"Is it – " she began; but he checked her.

"Nothing for you to worry over, my dear."

"What is it?" Dr Gordon demanded.

"Cowpox!"

"*Cowpox!*" It was a trio.

"Cowpox – that, and nothing else."

"But – what exactly is that?" the Head asked.

"Well, I suppose you might say that it's something between smallpox and chickenpox. I don't wonder you didn't recognise it, Gordon. Cases are very few and far between these days. I've just cleared up a small outbreak in my own practice, so the moment I saw it, I knew it for what it was. Keep Janice quiet and on a light diet, Nurse. See that she doesn't scratch. Not much else to do. Don't look so down, Gordon. I'll bet *you* never saw a case before, and with smallpox scares over half Europe, it was the natural thing to think. I'll be here for a few days, so if you don't object, I'll keep an eye on her. But there's no need for anyone to worry about her – thank heaven!"

As he said, so it was. Next morning saw the temperature dropped further, and thereafter Janice made steady progress, much to the relief of all concerned. The staff heaved a concerted sigh of relief and gave their minds fully to their proper work. The girls, thankful to know that all was well, attended to their usual summer-term ploys. Judy and Ailie ceased to walk round looking, as Margot had observed, like a couple of funeral mutes. As for Janice, she was quickly fretful and irritable, a sure sign of convalescence, as Nurse said. When that happened, Dr Chester said goodbye and returned to his work looking considerably more cheerful than he had done when he came.

As a result of all this, Miss Annersley was invited to attend a prefect's meeting one afternoon. The weather was hot and they held it in the rock garden which was, accordingly, barred to everyone else.

"Well, what is it?" she asked when she was comfortably settled.

"It's the Sale," Maeve said. "What are we to do about it? It's usually over by this time, but of course, with Janice being ill like that, we couldn't worry you about it. Thank goodness it *wasn't* smallpox!"

"Thank goodness, indeed!" the Head said gravely. Then she turned to the question of the Sale. "About the Sale, Maeve, I hardly know what to say. The exams begin in less than ten days. That would mean having the Sale this weekend and this is Wednesday. My dear girl, I don't think we could do it!"

They were fully agreed on this point. The Sale was the big event of the summer term and they had no mind to fall beneath the standard set in previous years.

"I suppose we'll have to have it after the exams," Maeve said.

"How far have you got in your plans?" the Head queried.

"Well, you know we decided to make it a Spanish Sale. We can manage the dresses and some of the art people have been scene-painting for dear life. You see, we want to show the Moorish side of Spain as well as the other. We're borrowing Herr Grauber's two donkeys and they will add to – to – "

"To the verisimilitude of the settings," put in Heather Clayton, saucily.

" – besides raising money with donkey-rides for any youngsters," Maeve continued, unperturbed.

"VA are repeating *The Little Germaine* as one of the entertainments," Len added, "and as that will take up the whole form, they're handing over all their stuff to VB for *their* stall. Luckily, those two forms were both doing needlework, so it fits in very nicely."

"And Lizette is arranging a concert," Maeve went on.

Lizette nodded. "It will be an hour long, and I thought if we gave it in the morning, we could repeat it in the afternoon."

"A good idea," Miss Annersley agreed. "Anything more?"

"Competitions," quiet Rosamund Lilley took her turn. "There will be clock-golf for the men as usual, and we have guessing the weight of Frau Mieders' cake. Then Suzanne Kiefen, Betty Landon, Hilda Pinosch and Ted Grantley are doing a book-titles competition on new lines."

"*What* new lines?" Heather demanded. "This is news to me."

"Well, instead of doing rhymes, they're making pictures to represent the titles – for instance, one picture is *Oliver Twist*." Rosamund began to giggle. "They've drawn a corkscrew."

"A *corkscrew?*" Even the Head exclaimed at that. "But how – "

"All – over – twist," Rosamund tried to look demure, but her eyes were dancing with laughter.

"Awful – awful!" Len cried. "Whoever evolved *that* ghastly pun ought to be hanged, drawn and quartered!"

"Who was it?" Alicia Leonard asked.

"I've no idea. They've kept *that* very dark!"

"They would!" Maeve spoke with conviction. "We'd better vet this affair before it's open to the public. Well then, Rosamund had a letter from Tom Gay and Tom says she's sending her usual contribution – only it's not exactly a *house* this time."

"Didn't she tell you what it was?" the head asked curiously. Tom Gay, an Old Chaletian, was famed for her magnificent dolls-houses. She sent one each year with a competition attached and each one had brought in a handsome sum.

Rosamund shook her head. "Not the least hint – drat her!" she added fervently. "All she did say was that for once she hadn't had to scratch round for the competition, for her offering made its own comp."

Miss Annersley laughed. "Tom does like to keep us on tenterhooks! Well, have you planned anything else in that line?"

"Not so far," Maeve owned. "We couldn't think of anything we hadn't done to death already."

"I think you must find one or two more. Competitions are always popular and they usually raise a good sum for us."

"Could *you* think of one?" Len suggested.

"I might. I'll do my best, anyhow. And what about draws?"

"They'll be all right. We have at least a dozen good ones already, including a set of lovely Bohemian wine glasses that Irma Ancocksy sent Mother," Len said. "Oh, and a gorgeous Spanish shawl Mother herself unearthed from one of the cases we'd still not opened since we came out here."

"Well, that sounds all right; but you know, girls, unless we can fit the Sale into the last fortnight of term, I'm afraid it must be put off till after the holidays."

There was a chorus of dismay at this.

"Oh, *not* next term!" Maeve cried. "A lot of us won't be here then, me included."

"Besides," Len added quickly, "We have the Nativity Play next term. We don't want our two biggest events in the one term, do we?"

"Oh, my dears, I agree with all you say, but unless we have Sports Day on the last Saturday but one and hold the Sale the following Saturday, I don't see how we're to – yes, Miss Dene?" for Rosalie Dene had come running down the steps to them, a paper in her hand which she gave to the Head.

"A cable, Miss Annersley."

The Head glanced at it and her face changed. "Oh – oh *no!*" She looked quickly at the prefects. "I'm sorry, girls. I must leave you. Arrange things to suit yourselves. The Sale is always your own affair, after all. I'm coming, Rosalie; I'll join you in the study. Girls, don't speak of this, please, to anyone." She left them on the word, hurrying after the secretary who was already halfway up the steps.

Left alone, the prefects looked at each other in some apprehension.

"What's up?" Monica Caird demanded.

No one could tell her. They discussed it briefly. Then Maeve clapped her hands.

"Stop it, all of you! It's the Head's business, when all's said and done. You turn your powerful minds to this Sale question. *Is* it to be the last Saturday or not? We'll vote on it and see how it goes. Slips, please, and don't forget that we *all* want to be in on it and some of us leave at the end of term and won't be available next. Get down to it!"

CHAPTER 16

Cable from Australia

In the study the Head shot the "Engaged' notice into place, locked the communicating-door with the office and then sat down in her chair. Her face was white and Rosalie Dene looked at her anxiously.

"You all right, Hilda? Would you like a dose of something?"

"No – no! I'm all right! Rosalie, what *shall* we do? How am I to break the news to that poor child?"

"Sir William says not to," Rosalie bent to point out the line.

"I can't help what he says. How does he think we can possibly keep it from her for more than twenty-four hours? Quite apart from his own fame, Lady Carew is famous in her own right as Daphne Cibber. It'll be in all the papers and on the radio as well."

"I hadn't thought of that. You're right, of course; we *can't* keep it from her. Even if we kept the papers from the Middles and unhitched their radio, the Seniors would hear. Girls are careless creatures and Jane is quick. She's happy here, but I know that a large part of her heart is in Australia. The merest hint and she'd be on it like lightning!"

"Apart from that, I don't agree that she should be kept in ignorance." Miss Annersley's lips set in a straight line. "If anything should – happen – if Lady Carew should – die – the shock would be terrible. I know what I'm talking about, Rosalie. I went through that experience myself at

163

Jane's age. My mother was ill for weeks before she died and no one told me anything. The first I knew of it was when my eldest brother came to fetch me home. I've never forgotten how I felt. I won't permit another child to go through that if I can prevent it."

"I think you're right." Rosalie spoke slowly. "It was shock enough when my own mother died and I was a grown-up girl then; it was so sudden, such a short illness, that there was no time to prepare anyone."

"And Jane is a sensitive youngster – almost supersensitive." The Head sat thinking for a moment. "Rosalie, get the San and tell Jack I must speak to him. Joey's down in Berne today, but Jack should be available."

Rosalie went into the office and while she was ringing the Sanatorium, Hilda Annersley read the cable again.

"I wish it said more," she thought. "But – 'Serious car accident. My wife in hospital in Sydney with multiple and dangerous injuries. Say nothing to Jane.' That may mean anything."

The San came through at that moment, and she thankfully turned to Jack Maynard for help. She read him the cable and he whistled briefly.

"What do you want me to do?" he asked.

"Get on to Jem on the radio phone and ask him for full details. I must know as far as possible exactly how matters stand."

"Can do. What about Jane?"

"Nothing for the moment. If possible, I'd like her to get her night's sleep first. But she's going to be told, Sir William to the contrary! She shall not have the awful shock of hearing she's motherless – if it comes to that and pray God it won't! – without some sort of preparation."

"O.K. I'll put in a call at once. Jem's in Sydney at the moment, so he'll be able to find out all there is to know."

"What a mercy! Ring me as soon as you've got through and tell me what he says. Oh, I wish Joey hadn't been inspired to go off to Berne today!"

"But she hasn't. Oh, I know she said she was going, but Geoff woke up early this morning with a tummy upset, so that put paid to Joey's expedition. She's at home this minute. Geoff? He's all right again. The heat and too much fruit accounted for him. If you want Jo, she'll come at once."

"I'll wait until you've heard from Jem. Jane knows nothing, of course, and no one is likely to tell her today, at any rate."

"O.K. You hang up and I'll fix that call. Try not to worry, Hilda."

He rang off and the Head considered a minute. Rosalie Dene was standing in the doorway, watching her with a harassed look. Miss Annersley relaxed a little.

"Don't look so worried, Rosalie. Jack's going to cope and, thank goodness, Joey's on tap if we need her. Geoff had a tummy upset, so she didn't go down. Now what measure shall we take? There'll be nothing in the papers yet, of course, and tomorrow, don't distribute them until I tell you. The radio's another matter. Silence the lot, will you? We'll run no risks. Out-of-order notices on each one, please, and I'll get Gaudenz to remove the plugs at once. Where is he?"

"Somewhere outside. I'll hunt him up myself and give him your message."

"Thanks; that ought to save trouble tonight. I'll go over and see Joey while you do that. She'll come if we want her. I remember Nell Wilson telling me how she comforted Jacynth Hardy when her aunt died."[1]

[1] *Gay from China.*

"And Mary-Lou Trelawney when the last news of her father came,"[1] Rosalie added.

The Head smiled faintly. "It wasn't exactly comfort Mary-Lou wanted but reassurance that she wasn't unnatural by not being heart-broken over his death. Poor Mary-Lou! She wasn't much more than a baby and she barely remembered him, so there was nothing unnatural about it, as Joey pointed out. I'm hoping Lady Carew may come through, but if she doesn't, then I want Joey at hand."

Rosalie nodded. "We would all do our best to help Jane if it came to the worst, but Joey has something very few other folk I've known have. She was the only person who really helped me when *my* mother died."

Thanks to these precautions, the day passed much as usual, and when bedtime came, Jane went off with the rest, unaware of any sorrow that might be coming to her. But not even Miss Annersley could prevent outside gossip.

The next afternoon, both IVA and B had games. The School grounds were fenced off from the rest of the Platz, but two of the tennis courts were near the road and visitors to the Platz very often stopped to watch the girls playing. Jane and three others were sent to one of these, with Heather Clayton as coach to her four and another on the next court. Miss Burnett was busy with beginners on two others and Monica Caird had departed with twenty-two eager people for a cricket practice. Len Maynard was in charge at the practice-boards with Rosamund Lilley to back her up.

Aimée Robinet came to Heather with a message and paused to watch Jane's four.

"Adrienne Didier is improving, n'est-ce-pas?" she

---

[1] *Three Go to the Chalet School.*

remarked as Adrienne took a tricky ball neatly and put it over right out of Jane's reach.

"Very promising," Heather agreed. then she shouted, "Dilys! You're footfaulting again! Watch it! That's the fourth time this set!" Dilys flushed. "No! Take that service again and do watch your feet!"

Dilys served with due care, but a moment later Heather was calling correction again – to Jane, this time. "Jane Carew, don't poach! That was Dilys' ball!"

Heather's voice was clear and carrying and her words reached two people who had paused to watch the game. They looked at each other with startled expressions as Adrienne drove to Dilys, who missed, giving the set to Adrienne and her partner. The four, mopping their hot faces, left the court and were sent to the boards, after Heather had criticised their play, to send up four more and, after a rest, to practice at their weak points.

Jack Lambert had come racing up at that moment with a message from Monica. Seeing Heather fully engaged, she stood to one side, leaning against the fence until the prefect could attend to her. As a result, she heard every word the strangers uttered.

"Jane Carew!" said one of them. "that must be Sir William Carew's only child. I heard she was at school in Switzerland, poor child!"

"It's a ghastly thing to have happened," remarked her companion, a young woman in her early twenties. "The driver was thrown more or less clear, wasn't she? And the other passenger only sustained a broken collar-bone. Isn't that what they said over the radio?"

"It is. What a pity Lady Carew was sitting in the back! She might have escaped then. It was a lorry running into them from behind, wasn't it?"

"I believe so. I know they said the lorry driver was

badly hurt, but that Lady Carew was the only one in real danger because she had been crushed against the back of the front seat and there were grave internal injuries."

"It's horrible! I do think something should be done about all these road accidents. They get worse and worse. I wonder if they've told the girl?"

"Didn't look like it. She was as jolly and cheery as anyone else."

"Poor child! How dreadful if her mother should die – and at such a distance from her!"

"The School will cope, I expect. Oh, how hot it is! Let's go and see if we can find a cold drink, shall we?"

They moved on, leaving a stunned Jack gripping the fence and, when Heather called to ask what she wanted, quite unable to give a clear message.

Heather impatiently sent her back to Monica to repeat it again and turned her attention to the new four who had come racing up. She was doing her best to work these Junior Middles up. Next term, as she knew, she would be Head of the games herself and she meant to have a good showing if she could.

Jack went tearing back to Monica, who scribbled a note after making a few trenchant remarks on her memory. Jack brought it, but Heather was too busy to notice her junior's dazed expression. She ordered Jack back to her cricket and thought no more about her.

Jack went, but only as far as the pavilion. With a quick glance over her shoulder, she made sure that Heather was not watching and then slipped into the pavilion where she marched into the changing-room and sat down to think.

"Something's happened to her mother," she thought. "A car accident. She can't know – she was laughing like anything when she went off with Adrienne. Does the Head know? Surely someone would tell her! Then why hasn't she told Jane? What should I do? I can't tell her myself – I just *can't!* Should I go to the Head or what? Oh, I *wish* those two hadn't yelled like that!"

Jack would probably have stayed there, trying to make up her mind, but at that point, Jane herself burst into the changing-room to pick up the woolly she had forgotten to take with her when she left the court.

"Jack!" she exclaimed, when she saw Jack. "Is this where you are? Monica was shrieking for you a few minutes ago." She saw the other girl's white face and came nearer. "Is anything the matter? Oh, my dear, do you feel ill? You look simply awful! Shall I fetch someone, Jack? I won't be a minute. Look, you lie down on the lockers and I'll fly for someone. You'll be all right!"

She took Jack's arm to help her over to the lockers, but Jack resisted.

"It's all right. I'm OK I'm not ill or anything!" she burst out.

"But you do look ghastly," Jane persisted. "I'm sure you should lie down or something. Do let me go and fetch someone, Jack!"

"I tell you I'm as fit as anything!" Jack snapped. Then, more gently, "Honestly, Jane, there's not a thing the matter with me."

She so obviously meant it, that Jane had to believe her – and jumped to a fresh conclusion. "Jack! You – you haven't had bad news, have you?"

Jack lost her head. "No, not for me – "

"Bad news for someone else, then? I'm so awfully sorry – " She stopped short and stared at Jack in silence, her eyes beginning to darken with horror. As Rosalie Dene had said, she was quick. Something about Jack told her that the bad news was for her. Before the aghast Jack

169

could say or do anything, Jane's hands were gripping her arms so tightly that it hurt.

"Jack! Do you mean – is there – is it from – Australia?"

Jack shook her head. She was literally unable at that moment to speak.

Jane shook her violently. "Tell me – *tell me!* What is it? Is it Mother? Or Father? Jack! You *must* tell me!"

Jack made an effort. Wrenching herself free, she said, "I – I *can't* tell you, Jane." With a sudden inspiration she added, "Go to the Head! *She'll* tell you! Go on – I mean it."

Jane's hands had dropped. She was white and shaking as she leaned against the nearby wall. Instinctively, Jack caught her and flung an arm round her to steady her.

"Jane!" she said urgently. "Buck up! Get hold of yourself! I'll go with you to the Head if you like. but I can't tell you myself. I – I haven't any right, anyhow. It was just – something I – overheard."

Jane swallowed hard, still leaning against her. "Tell me this, then. Is it – is it – *bad?*" Her voice shook and Jack, everything that had gone before forgotten just then, hugged her.

"No one's dead, if that's what you're thinking. I can tell you that, anyhow. It's an accident and you never know much about that till you've heard how it happened. The Head will know. They'd cable her at once. Come on and I'll take you to her! Keep you chin up! It never helps to go under for anything!" Clumsily as any boy, she kissed the nearest part of Jane's anatomy – an ear – and then repeated, "Chin up! Things always look beastly when you only know bits. The Head'll be able to tell you."

"I'll come," Jane whispered. Then, "Can we – I don't want to see anyone but the Head – not any of the girls, I mean."

Jack thought swiftly. "We can climb over the fence and go up the road and turn in at the drive. They mightn't see us then. Come on! I'll help you over."

That this was a flat breaking of a strict rule, she neither heeded nor cared, and all Jane could think of was her parents. She was still trembling, but Jack's injunction to keep her chin up had got through. She set her teeth, forced herself to be steady and went with Jack, though terror had dimmed her eyes and she went like a sleep-walker.

Jack led her out of the back-door to the pavilion. The fence lay just behind and no one saw them scramble over it. The bell rang for the end of the period, but neither heard it. Jack was too absorbed in getting Jane safely to the study and Jane herself was too stunned by fear to hear anything or do anything but stumble along, helped by the arm Jack kept round her.

No one saw them either in the road or the drive and Jack knew better than to go round to their usual entrance. She boldly took Jane in by the front door and to the study by means of a little passage more or less sacred to the Head.

As they reached the study, the door opened and Miss Annersley herself appeared. Behind her was Joey who had slipped over, once her babies were put down for their nap, to plan with her how Jane was to be told. The Head glanced quickly from one agitated girl to the other, but Joey was quicker still.

Slipping past Miss Annersley, she took Jane from Jack. "All right, Jack! Off you go and keep a still tongue, please. I'll see you later." Then, "Jane my lamb, let go of Jack. We'll tell you everything you want to know."

Jane looked up into eyes that were soft as black pansies. Jack had loosed her hold, but she was in stronger arms now and a warm, motherly sympathy was flowing all round her, helping to ease a little of that horrible fear. Jack slid away without realising it, and Joey and the Head drew her into the study and shut the door.

Jane looked up again. "Which?" she half-whispered.

"Your mother, my lamb. She's been badly hurt in a motor accident. They took her to a hospital in Sydney and last night they operated on her. That's all the news we have at present, though Dr Jack is ringing up this minute to hear how she is and as soon as he knows, you'll be told."

Jane stared at her, sheet-white. "It – she – she – "

"No, my darling!" Joey was at her most motherly. She held the stunned girl closely to her. "She is living, but very badly hurt and they couldn't tell us how things would go. the operation was a success in itself, but it all depends on how she comes through in the next few hours."

Jane suddenly shook herself free and though she was still white, her eyes had come to life. "We're wasting time! I must go to her at once! I can fly! Father wouldn't mind the expense. If I fly I can be there in a day or two!"

"Not yet," the Head said quietly. "We must wait a little longer, Jane, until we hear again. As soon as we do and if your father agrees, we'll make all arrangements to get you the first available seat on a plane."

"But I *must* go to her!" Jane cried wildly. "She's my mother – she'll want me! I must go to her! You're cruel to try and make me wait! I *must* go, I tell you – I *must*!"

She made a dash for the door, but the Head had turned the key and she twisted the knob fruitlessly. The telephone rang sharply and Miss Annersley went to answer it. Rosalie Dene had gone down to Berne, to find out the quickest plane to Sydney if Jane had to go. As she shut the door, Joey came and pulled Jane's hands away from the door knob.

"Jane!" she said severely. "Pull yourself together at once! A lot of use you'll be to anyone, sick or well, if you go on in this hysterical way! Stop it, I say! Stop it at once!"

The sharpness got through to Jane and checked the rising hysteria. For a moment she stood staring dumbly at Joey. The she gave a cry and burst into tears. Joey lifted her and, big girl as she was, carried her across the room and sat down in the Head's big armchair, cradling her as if she were little Cecil.

"That's better!" she said, only tenderness in her voice now. "That's right, Jane-girl! Cry as hard as you like. You'll feel better soon. There – there!"

She sat holding Jane, stroking the fair head and murmuring softly to her. Jane clung to her and sobbed and shook, great tears pouring down and soaking Joey's frock right through. She slipped her own clean handkerchief into the hot hand and sat quietly, waiting until the tears should lessen, but too wise to try to check them at once. Then the Head returned and came to lift the fair head so that she could look down into the swollen eyes.

"I've better news for you, Jane. Can you listen, dear? That was Dr Jem – Sir James Russell, Mrs Maynard's brother-in-law – on the radio-phone. He has been to the hospital – he was ringing from there. Listen, Jane! Your mother recovered consciousness a few minutes ago and they are more hopeful. Dr Jem says she has come through the operation in better shape than they had feared. She is still very ill, but she has a real chance now. And Jane, Dr Jem really *knows*. He said, 'Tell Jane that though it will probably be very slow, I think myself her mother will pull through'. And he *knows!*"

Jane took it in slowly. She was worn out with shock and crying and it took time for her to grasp the greater hope. The Head repeated the message twice more and she got it at last.

"That's true?" she asked.

"Quite true, dear. Your mother isn't out of the wood yet, but there is every reason to hope that she soon will be."

"Th-thank you!" Tears stood in the grey eyes, but Jane was too exhausted even to cry now. Joey acted quickly. Rising, she set Jane on her feet, still keeping an arm round her.

"And now, you're coming home with me and going to bed. You shall have some milk and then you'll go to sleep and when you wake up again, there'll be still better news for you. Come along, precious! Your bed's all ready and waiting."

Of what came next, Jane never remembered anything. Joey and the Head took her between them to Freudesheim where she was undressed and put to bed. A beaker of milk into which Joey had slipped something her husband had left her was swallowed down, and then she was laid down and ten minutes later the two watching her heard her quiet breathing and knew she was asleep.

"I'll leave her to you." Hilda Annersley got up from her chair. "Let me know how she is about midnight, Joey. Ring for me if you want me."

"I will, but I doubt if it'll be necessary. She's worn out, poor kid, and she's had Jack's sedative. She'll probably sleep the clock round."

Joey glanced round and then followed her friend from the room.

"If there's any change over there," Miss Annersley said

as they parted for the night, "Jem will ring us. But he doesn't expect it."

Then she went back to the school to be met by a deeply penitent Jack who confessed to all her sins where Jane was concerned, including coming back to school by the road. The Head said very little to her, either in the way of blame or consolation, but one thing she did say which Jack remembered.

"Lady Carew's accident had nothing to do with you, Jack. But you *have* been greatly to blame for not fighting your silly ill-feeling towards Jane. I'm glad that you have overcome it now for her sake and your own. That is all. Punish you for breaking the rules? No; I think you had punishment enough. Go now, and make up your mind that never again will you let yourself give way to such foolish and wrong ideas."

Jack went with a very hangdog air. The Head turned to Rosalie Dene who had come in just then and, for the first time since the news had come, smiled. "Poor Jack! Still, feeling herself what she calls 'a specious pig' and repenting for dear life of her many sins won't hurt her. In fact, this looks to me like a turning-point for her. Jack will make all the finer woman for her present bitter regret, so I'm not sorry for her really. And oh, thank God it looks as if Lady Carew has a real chance now!"

CHAPTER 17

Jane Has to be Patient

"Jane! Wake up! I've news for you!"

Jane rolled over on her back and stared straight up into Joey Maynard's black eyes, which were glowing. For a moment she couldn't imagine why Mrs Maynard should be in her cubicle. Then memory flooded back and she sat up.

"You mean you've heard again? How is she? What does Father say?"

"Not your father, lamb, but Dr Jem – a cable. Here you are!" Joey put the cable into Jane's hands and went to pick up the tray she had deposited on the table.

Jane read it avidly. " 'Improvement maintained.' " She looked up at Joey. "That mean's she really is getting better, doesn't it?"

Joey set the tray down on her knees. "It does! She's holding her own and at this stage, every hour is a gain. Oh, Jane, I'm so *glad* for you! And now, here's your breakfast. I'll just tuck this cushion behind you and then you'll be all right, won't you?"

She tucked the cushion firmly behind Jane's back, poured out the coffee and then kissed the broad brow lightly.

Jane looked up with eyes full of appreciation. "Oh, you are *kind!*"

"Then you reward me by clearing all those dishes!" Joey retorted gaily. She had more news for Jane, but knew better than to give it until the girl had had a meal.

176

She waited until the poached egg, the triangles of golden-brown toast loaded with butter and honey, and the delicious coffee had all vanished. Then she took the tray away and came to sit on the side of the bed.

"More news, Jane! Today, you and your father are having a brief – a *very* brief – chat on the 'phone! How's that?"

"Talk to Father? Do you *mean* it?" Jane's eyes shone.

"I do; your father's coming through about midday with any luck. You'll get information straight from the horse's mouth, so to speak."

"Oh, how *marvellous!*" Then, at Joey's quizzical look, "Well, I do mean that. It *is* marvellous!"

"All right; we'll let it go for once. Now what about a bath? Come along and I'll show you the bathroom. Matey sent over a change for you and your toilet articles, too. Come along, and when you're ready, trot downstairs. I'll be in the salon." And Joey picked up the tray, led Jane to the bathroom and went off, duty-bound, while her guest took a good bath and then scuttered back to her room to dress. Half an hour later, she came down looking more like herself, though there were still shadows under her eyes and she was paler than usual.

"Where am I to take the call?" she asked eagerly when Joey had set her to work, helping to dust the attractive salon.

"In my study. We decided it would be more private than at school. After it's over, you can either go back or you can stay here for the rest of the day. It's up to you to decide. Oh, not now. Wait until you hear what your father has to say. Here comes Dr Jack! Jack, do you want coffee?"

"I wouldn't say no to it," the doctor replied. "Hello, Jane! Feeling better? Good! You've only another hour to wait and then you'll have all your dad's news. It'll be short, I'm afraid. The radio-telephone isn't exactly cheap. But at least you'll have heard all he has to say – ah, thanks, Joey!" as she brought him a big cup of creamy coffee. "Babies all right?"

"Quite – in fact Geoff seems to be making up for yesterday." Joey said ruefully. "He threw his mug at Rösli and it was the world's work to get him to take his morning nap. Still, he's well away now, thank goodness!"

"Little demon!" the doctor said with a grin.

Jane was looking at him eagerly. "Dr Jack!"

"Yes?"

"You do think Mother will really get well now, don't you?"

Jack knew better than to build much on the frail foundation which was all they had so far, but neither could he dampen the girl's spirits. "It looks like it," he agreed. "It'll be slow, Jane, and you'll have to be patient. But if she goes on making progress, yes; sooner or later she should be her old self again."

"What was it exactly? Do you know?"

"A skidding lorry crashed into the back of the car in which she was travelling with two friends. A Mrs Tracey was driving and she got off with cuts and bruises and shock. A Miss Sanderson, also in front, broke her collarbone and was pretty badly shocked. They're both making headway now, though. Your mother, in the back, was caught between the back of the front seat and the back of the car, which was crushed in. She broke three ribs, which didn't matter so much; the major trouble was internal injuries. They had to operate at once or she would have died. However, she's evidently standing up to the after-effects of a major operation and double shock. The big question was whether her heart would hold out. It's two days since it happened and not only is she living, but she is making progress, however slow. So I think you may hope for the best now, little maid."

"Thank you," Jane said soberly. "I wanted to know."

"Yes; that was your right. I've told you the whole thing because that's your right, too. You may believe me, Jane, when I tell you to hope. I wouldn't try to cheat you. The Chalet School believes in training girls to become strong, helpful women, not spineless creatures who can't take anything. So I don't say your mother is out of danger yet – she isn't. But you can take that."

"I can take anything if only Mother gets all right in the end," Jane asserted.

"You can! And Jane! If things seem to be too hard – and that may happen sometimes – come to us. Joey is unofficial mother to every girl in the school who needs it. She calls herself one of the School's foundation stones and says she'll always be a Chaletian, even if she lives to be a centenarian with great-great-grandchildren clamped round her knees to hear her tales of the School's early days!"

Jane relaxed and laughed at this touching picture as he meant her to do. "It does sound Methuselah-ish!" she said. "And – and if ever I *do* need help, I'll come all right. But I'm going to hang on and hope as hard as I can."

"Good! And Jane, There's one other thing you can do."

"Oh, what's that?" Jane looked up eagerly.

"*Pray* for your mother. God's awfully good to us, but he does like us to ask Him for help – just as your dad likes you to come to me. We're all fathers. He is the great All Father. Understand?"

"Yes; and I have – I do!"

"And," Joey put in, "when things are all right again, for goodness sake don't forget to say 'Thank You!'" either. You've no more right to be rude to God than to anyone else."

This was an unexpected point of view for Jane; but she saw it at once.

"I never thought about forgetting to say 'Thank You' being *rude*. But it is, of course. I'll remember," she promised. Then she changed the subject. "Dr Jack, do you think they'll let me fly to Sydney straight away?"

"That depends on your dad, my child. If he says you must wait till the end of term, that will be that. You can take that, too."

Jane looked doubtful. "I'm not so sure. I'll try. But oh, I hope he'll say I can go!"

"Naturally; but I don't advise you to be too hopeful about *that!*" Jack said. He had his own ideas about what Sir William would say.

"You people had better hop along to the study," Joey broke in. "It's getting on for midday – only five minutes to go now. By the way, Jane, I hope you'll be able to hear all right. Sometimes the atmospherics are a complete curse!"

Actually, there was very little bother with atmospherics for once. The call came through with amazingly little delay. Jack handed the receiver to the excited Jane and left her to it.

"That you, Janekin?"

"Oh, Fardy!" Jane resorted to her baby name for him. "How wonderful to hear you! How's Mother?"

"Improving steadily, though very slowly, of course. She's still too ill to have even me as a visitor. I've only been allowed to peep at her when she's asleep. But, thank God, they all say they think she'll make it now."

"Oh, Fardy – Fardy! How too marvellous! Oh, I'm so thankful!"

"So well you may be!" The beautiful, trained actor's voice shook a little. "At one time it was touch and go with her. But it's different now."

"Can I come to you as soon as there's a vacant seat on a plane?"

"No, Janie. Sorry, darling, but it can't be done. For one thing, if you did come they wouldn't let you see her for some time yet. Everything depends on her being quiet and with no excitement. For another, I don't want you here until there's someone to keep an eye on you. At present, there isn't. I couldn't leave you by yourself in a hotel. But by the end of your term, Lady Russell, who is visiting an old friend in Tasmania at the moment, will be back, and you're going there so as to be near to Mother. That's – how long?"

"F-five weeks," Jane faltered, as she worked out the answer to the question.

"Right! Your Head will make arrangements for you to fly out the day you break up and I promise you that by that time you'll be able to visit Mother every day and for quite long visits, too. Meantime, it's your job to hold the fort where you are. It's your share of the price we must pay for Mother's recovery. Is it too heavy, my pet?"

"Oh, no – no! If it has to be that way, I can take it – and gladly!"

"That's my girl!"

"And Fardy, you don't have to worry about me, either. Mrs Maynard will help me if things get too hard!"

"Blessings on her! Now, Janie-girl, I must ring off. Chin up, old lady! Remember you're a Carew! 'Strong to endure' – that's the family motto. See you live up to it! Mother really will be as fit as ever, even though it may

181

take a long time. Hang on to that and be brave! Bless you, my girlie!"

"Yes; goodbye, Fardy! Give Mother all my love as soon as you can!"

The call ended and Jane hung up. For a moment she remained in her chair, elbows on the table, chin buried in her hands. Finally, she stood up and shook herself. "It won't be easy, but I'm not a baby. I can take it if I've got to. And oh, thank God – *thank God* she'll be really well again some day!"

With a memory of Joey Maynard's words, she dropped on her knees to say a special "Thank You!" Jack, looking in, saw her, but before he could vanish again, she glanced up and saw him.

"I was only thanking God," she said simply. "I've got to stay till the end of term, but I can take it all right just as you said. Mother is getting better and oh, when I think she mightn't be here at all, I do feel I can take *anything* that comes!"

"Of course you can," he said as he lifted her to her feet. "You're not a weak-kneed coward but a girl with a backbone. You go back to school and pitch in at work and play and you'll be surprised at the way the time will go. Term-end isn't so far off and then it'll be hey for Australia and your mother! By the way, you aren't flying alone or even with strangers. Our Margot is off to spend the holidays with a great chum who lives at Manly. Emmy and her dad are coming to pick her and you up and they'll see to everything. You'll come back with Margot, too. Emmy has left school now, being grown-up – or supposed to be. And my sister-in-law's will be home for you and for your mother, too, when she leaves hospital. She's cabled to say so. Now come along back to Joey. After

182

lunch you can run back to school and get down to having a really good report to show when you get there."

"Oh, how *marvellous* it will be!" Jane breathed as she followed him to the salon. "It's going to be worth everything in the end – I can see that!"

CHAPTER 18

The End of a Feud

Jane had said she could take anything now that she knew that her mother had a chance of full recovery; but the shock had made a change in her. For the time being much of her verve and gaiety had gone and the Middles hardly knew their eager Jane in this quiet girl who seemed to have little to say except about school affairs, and whose laughter came so rarely.

"You know," Dilys remarked one day when Jane had gone off for a Latin coaching, "I do miss her – her *whirlwindiness!* She used to be always on the go and now she's different."

"But that is to be expected," Adrienne told her.

"Yes, but Lady Carew is getting better now – *really* better. You know what the Head told us at Prayers this morning. She can have visitors for ten minutes at a time and she's begun to send Jane her own messages. That shows you!" Jean chimed in. "I wish Jane would buck up! She's not like herself at all."

Other people had noticed it, among them Jack Lambert. Jack was not given to much really deep thinking except at long intervals. However, on this particular Saturday, the day was so scorching that instead of their usual ramble or games, they were told they must be content to remain quietly in the school grounds. If the evening were cooler, they might have tennis or cricket; but the afternoon must be spent as tranquilly as possible.

After Mittagessen, where Karen had served everything

184

iced that could be iced, they got their books and needle-work and scattered to seek what shade was to be found under the big pines and firs. The Juniors were ordered off to their dormitories where they stripped, pulled on their dressing-gowns, and lay down on their beds with every door and window set wide open. Some of the Junior Middles went too. Wanda and the rest of Jack's gang sought out nooks and corners in twos and threes and it must be owned that more than half of them fell asleep over their books.

Jack, with Wanda, Val, Margaret Twiss and the two Dutch girls, was sprawling in the shade of a giant juniper bush with an abridged version of *Barnaby Rudge* beside her. No lover of books, she soon dropped it and got up.

"Where are you going?" Val asked her lazily.

"Somewhere cooler – if I can find it."

"What a hope! It's as cool here as anywhere. Sit down, Jack, and don't be such an ass!"

"Ass yourself!" Jack retorted, quitting them with a purposeful air.

"She is quite mad," Renata van Buren murmured.

Clad, like everyone else, in her sunsuit, Jack wandered off to the mass of bushes which bordered the path to Freudesheim. The heat striking out from the brick wall on the other side showed her that she would find no coolness there. She reached the gate and hung over it. A little way up the rising slope of the Freudesheim garden there was another clump of bushes. Jack, with complete disregard for rules, opened the gate, went through and curled herself up in what shade there was. Then she gave herself up to some serious thinking.

"I just don't understand," she thought. "*Why* have I hated Jane Carew so from the word go! It's mad!"

She stretched out, kicked her heels on the baked grass

and thought again. It *had* been a blow to be moved from Pansy, but she had got over that now. She and Len generally saw each other at least twice a week and Len was as ready as ever to answer her questions – when she could! Some of Jack's queries were odd, to say the least of it.

"It can't be because Jane and I aren't interested in the same things," she said, half-aloud. "Wanda couldn't care less about machinery and nor could most of the others; yet I'm pals with them. I do think the way she used to talk was quite mad, but after all it's no worse than lots of the others; only different, of course. And the way she helped me out of that tree was frightfully decent. The Head said we might both have been killed if any more boughs had broken." She broke off her train of thought. "Oh, gosh! She nearly skinned me that time! I've had some stiff tickings-off in my time, but I never want another like that! I only wonder I was able to get out of the study on my *feet* by the time she'd finished!"

"Jack Lambert! What on earth are you doing here?"

Jack came to herself with a start and looked up to see Len Maynard standing over her, looking very much the prefect. With a gasp she scrambled to her feet.

"What are you doing here?" Len repeated. "Had you leave?"

"Er – no," Jack replied.

"Well then?"

Jack scraped one toe along the grass. "I was hot – and the others *would* talk when I wanted to think – and it looked cool."

Len stopped looking official and laughed. "So you decided that rules could go hang – that it?"

"Well – er – "

Len sat down and pulled the younger girl down beside her. "I ought to send you to report – but I won't. Instead, you can tell me what's bothering you. Serious thought isn't much in your line yet, Jack. What's started you off on a boiling-hot day like this?"

"Oh, I don't know. 'S a matter-of-fact, I've been thinking rather a lot lately – well, ever since we heard about the accident to Jane's mother," Jack blurted out. "It sort of set me going."

"Something to do with Jane, then. Tell me, Jack. I might be able to help."

Jack eyed her doubtfully. "I'm all muddled up. I can't explain, exactly."

Len thought. This was a tricky business and she must handle it carefully.

"What really started your dislike of Jane?" she asked.

"Well, it was that dormy business in the beginning."

"Yes – so you said before. But I thought you'd got over that."

Jack considered. Then her defences collapsed. "It may sound mad, but actually, I have. Only – well, you see, I'd got into the way of disliking Jane, and I went on. I thought she was soppy – and rather mad. Only – and this is even madder – lately I've wondered if I couldn't quite like her if I let myself. I would, only – well, I'm not like most girls. I can't begin to go all over her. I wouldn't know what to say or how to begin."

Len smothered a grin at the idea of Jack "going all over' anyone.

"It wouldn't be you; that's certain," she agreed.

"No; only after the way she yanked me out of that tree – and I know now how jolly dangerous it was – you should have heard the Head about it when she got really going! – and she never seemed to think she'd done anything much or anything – and then, look how plucky she's been over this business of her mother's." Grammer was going to the winds with Jack's earnestness, but Len understood what she was after, which was the main thing. She let the younger girl go on unchecked and Jack warmed to her subject and found her constrained tongue free for once.

"I do admire the way Jane's taken it. Once, I'd have thought she'd be howling half the time and expecting everyone to ooze up round her. But she's not *been* like that. She's kept her chin up and she's scarcely said anything unless anyone asked her. She hasn't gone slack about things, either, but just carried on. I – I admire that sort of thing. There's a lot more in her than I thought and just lately I – well, I've wondered if we could be – well, not pals, exactly – well, it wasn't likely – I mean – well, if I said anything she might think – might think – "

Jack's normal reserve over emotional subjects tangled her tongue and she came to a full-stop, not very sure by this time just what she did feel.

"I see," Len said quietly. "You know, Jack, what's really happened is that you've got round to disliking not Jane, but the girl *you've* been where Jane was concerned. You'd like to make a fresh start, but haven't much chance of a straight talk with her in school; and you're afraid she may think that what you say is because you're sorry for her and you'd hate that yourself."

Jack stared at her, wide-eyed. "Gosh! How did you understand?"

"I just did. Now, my lamb, I'll see you get your chance, but I don't think you'd better pour all this out to Jane. You'd only end by muddling both of you and I agree that she'd probably hate any grand reconciliation as much as you. Now be quiet and let me think."

Jack rolled over with her back to Len, and Len clasped her hands round her knees and thought hard. Suddenly, she jumped to her feet. "I'm just flying home for a sec. You wait here until I come back," she commanded.

Flying was not exactly in order just then, but Len made haste. When she returned, she grinned broadly, for Jack, in an effort to keep cool, had pulled off her button-through frock and was lying fully spread-eagled on the grass.

"Cooler that way?" she inquired. "Well, pick up your frock and go on to the rose-garden and wait there till I come. Rösli and Anna have the babies in the shadiest corner, but there's plenty more shade in other corners. Hop it!"

Jack was on her feet. "Gosh, Len, I can't go to see your mother like this! I'm filthy!"

"OK We *have* a bathroom, you know – six, in fact! You go and find one and take a shower. That'll freshen you. Well, what is it?" for Jack was one large question-mark.

"It's just – I mean *six bathrooms!* It sounds *colossal!*"

Len went off into a peal of laughter. "Originally it was twelve, but we've made store-rooms of some of them. Did no one ever tell you that Freudesheim used to be a pension – the Pension Wellington, to be exact? That's the why of that one! Now you scram and go down to the rose-garden when you're through. Look in the cupboard and you'll find a towel and you can go to my bedroom and tidy your hair. You'll be all right then. Your frock's not too bad."

She gave Jack a shove in the direction of the house before she hurried off to the School. Jack stared after her, but went. All the doors were open and she had often visited Freudesheim. She found her bathroom and showered thoroughly and lengthily. In fact, she was still drying herself when Len's voice sounded outside the door.

189

"Open that door, Jack! I've brought you some fresh things. That sunsuit of yours was literally sticking to you!"

Jack obeyed and received a fresh sunsuit with matching top. She finished drying, pulled her garments on, went upstairs to Len's room where she brushed her wet hair into some sort of order and then, fairly cool for the first time since early morning, sauntered downstairs and out into the garden.

"Good old Len!" she thought. "She's so jolly decent the way she thinks of everything! And gosh! How she understands just how you feel, even when you can't get it clear in your own mind! I feel all tidied up now, inside as well as out."

She had reached the top of the steps by this time and she stood looking down. In the corner where there was a big patch of shade, Rösli and Anna had Cecil and the twins, who were playing about in tiny sunsuits, and were as brown as berries. In another corner was a small standing-hammock where Len was sitting with Jane. The elder girl had been keeping an eye open for Jack and she waved to her and called.

"Come on, Jack! Mother's mixing one of her patent fruit drinks and I want to go and help her. You and Jane can look after each other while I'm gone."

She got up, giving Jack an encouraging pat on the shoulder when she passed her and then Jack and Jane were together, eyeing each other uncertainly.

"Well, you look cool enough!" Jack said in offhand tones as she sat down in Len's place. "I say, I like your hair like that. Is it cooler?"

Jane nodded. "Len told me to do it and pinned it up for me. It feels quite firm and it's a lot cooler than having it all round my neck and ears."

"It looks it!"

"You look cool yourself. The last time I saw you – "

"I looked as I felt – like a boiled lobster!" Jack grinned. "I've had a shower and Len brought me some clean things. My hair's still wettish, but it'll soon dry in this heat."

"It's nearly dry already," Jane assured her.

Having exhausted that topic, they were silent. Then Jack spoke.

"Any news of your mother?"

Jane gaped at her. "But, my dear! The Head gave it out at Prayers! Didn't you hear? She's *much* better. Tomorrow, they're going to raise her in bed just a little. So far, they've had to keep her flat, but now they're lifting her and Father said in his cable that it was just the beginning."

"Smashing! I'm jolly glad! By the time term ends and you go to them, she ought to be sitting up in a chair."

"Oh, do you really think so?" Jane's voice was wistful. "I've been hoping; but she's been so terribly ill and I was afraid she mightn't be strong enough, even then."

"You bet she will! How are you going, by the way?"

"Oh, flying, of course! I'm going with Margot Maynard and some friends of hers. She's spending the hols with them at Manly, which is near Sydney. Father will meet me at the airfield, but actually, I'm to stay with Lady Russell and oh, Jack, as soon as Mother can leave hospital, she's going there as well. Isn't it *decent* of them? Lady Russell wrote to me. She's been to visit Mother since she came home from Tasmania and she said that though it wasn't likely she'd be there by the time I reached Australia, Sir Jem thought it wouldn't be many weeks later and we might have at least a month together there."

"Oh, good! But aren't you staying out there?"

Jane shook her head. "No; only for the hols. I'm coming back when Margot does."

"Oh? I wondered if they'd want to keep you with them."

"Oh, but darling, how could they? It's a tour and they don't stay long anywhere. Besides, Father said when he wrote that there was just a chance that Mother might come home some time in late October. She won't be fit to go on tour for ages, of course. Everyone says now that she *will* be all right in time, only – it's going to be rather a long time."

Jane's voice broke and her sensitive lips quivered.

"You'd expect that after a doing like that. It's only sense. Will she come out here, do you think? It's a magnificent place for people getting better."

"Here – do you mean to the Görnetz Platz? I hadn't thought of that. Jack, what a – a *miraculous* idea!" Jane was all animation now. "Of course, it's the very place for her! We'd be near each other and the air is marvellous. I'll suggest it when I write tomorrow. Honestly, Jack, that's an absolute inspiration! Thanks a million for suggesting it!"

"Well, it seems sensible to me," quoth Jack.

"Sensible? It's a stroke of genius! Only – where could she go?"

"Not a clue! Oh, yes I have. Ask Mrs Maynard. She'd know exactly where to fix her. What's more, she's on the spot and would see to it all." Jack spoke with supreme certainty. "Tell you what, Jane, we'll talk it over with Len first and she'll tell her mother and it'll all be settled quite easily."

"Oh, how marvellous it would be – "

"I say," Jack interrupted. "Mind if I tell you something?"

"Of course not! What is it?"

"Well, I wouldn't say 'marvellous' quite so much if I were you. They don't like it at School."

"Why ever not?" Jane's eyes were round.

"No idea. I just know they choke us off it if they hear us. I thought I'd better tell you."

"Of course! Thanks a lot! And thanks more than I can say for your mar – " Jane halted and Jack grinned.

"Call it 'fabulous'!" she suggested.

Jane laughed. "It sounds quite mad, but it'll do. Right! – fabulous ideas then!"

"Ass!" Jack said, smiting her on the back. "Nothing fabulous about it – just common sense! There's Len waving to us to go and help carry things." She jumped to her feet, caught Jane's hand and pulled her on to hers. "Come on! I'm not running for anybody today, but we'd better move a *little!*"

And that was all. There was no grand reconciliation scene; no apologies from anyone; not even an explanation. But thereafter, Jack and Jane were on friendly terms which deepened into genuine friendship as time went on, and this was good for them both.

CHAPTER 19

Joey Opens the Sale

"Maeve, *when* are we going to see Tom's house?" Ailie Russell looked up hopefully at her cousin and Maeve chuckled maddeningly.

"Not until it's all set out." She regarded with a grin Ailie's small pointed face framed in its halo of fair curls. At fifteen, the youngest of the Russell girls remained, like her mother, small and slight and looking two or three years younger than her actual age. "What a kid you look, Ailie! Now it's no use trying to coax me. I meant what I said."

"Oh, Maeve, you *are* a pig!" Ailie retorted. "And *I* can't help my size. Dad says I'm like Mummy – and the only one of us all who is."

"Not like her in colouring. Your mother has dark hair and brown eyes. But you Russells are all as bad as the Maynards. You come in every shade of colour. Now you just trot back to your stall and get on with it. It's far from ready yet or I miss my guess!"

"It's practically finished. Books don't take all that much setting out! We've only got them and jigsaws and table games and we've borrowed some bookcases and filled the shelves with books so that left only the jigsaws and games to worry about. Each shelf has books of the same price, so that people can see what they've got to pay for what without any trouble."

"That was a good idea," Maeve said. "Who hatched it?"

"Well – er – me," Ailie replied with becoming modesty.

"Maeve, *why* won't you let anyone have a sniff at Tom's house?"

"Because we want it to burst on you in its pristine beauty," Maeve responded sweetly. "I can tell you this – you'll all be thrilled to the brim when you see it. But that's all I'm saying at present – yes, Gaudenz?" as the big man came up to them. "What is it?"

"A box has arrived, mein Fräulein. It is addessed to you and is from England," he said, speaking in his native Swiss-German.

"Right! I'll come. Thank you, Gaudenz." He went off again and Maeve turned back to her cousin. "I must go, but get this and get it good. You're not seeing this latest affair of Tom's till you can all see it together. Now scram!"

Ailie went, after relieving her feelings by making a horrible face after Maeve's retreating back. Maeve, knowing nothing about it, went on her way unperturbed. She reached the screens set up round a certain corner of the garden and slipped behind them.

"Hello! Come on and help!" Len Maynard commanded.

"Can't! Gaudenz has just informed me that there's a box arrived for me from England so I must go and open it. Come on and help me, Monica, there's a lamb!"

Monica Caird put down the small doll she was holding. "OK! I say, Maeve, Tom's excelled herself this time, hasn't she?"

"She has! She once did an entire village for us – the Sale we had on St Briavel's just before we came out here – but it had nothing on this effort."[1]

---

[1] *Bride Leads the Chalet School.*

"I remember it. I thought it simply marvellous," Monica assented. "But you're right. This beats it into fits."

She cast an admiring glance at the long trestle table round which the members of VIA and B were gathered and it certainly was worth admiring.

It bore a long series of miniature houses, no two of which were alike. There was a Swiss chalet, a Chinese pagoda, a white-walled eastern house with a dome and an inner courtyard round which a cloister-like passage ran on all sides, an Eskimo igloo of beehive shape, painted white and with fine black lines tracing the shape of frozen snow-blocks, an English country cottage, complete with thatched roof, lattice windows and tiny climbing roses clinging to the walls and dangling over the rustic porch. There were many others, each belonging to a different land and all attractive to the last degree. They had all been set up and now the girls were busy disposing tiny dolls, dressed in the native costume of the country to which the house belonged, before each.

"Tom told me in her last letter that she had spent every moment of her spare time on it," Rosamund Lilley remarked as Maeve and Monica left them. "Of course, her boys helped on carpentry nights at the Club and the girls dressed the dolls."

"No need to tell us that last bit," Con Maynard said with a chuckle. "The day I see a doll dressed by Tom herself, prepare to catch me, for I shall certainly swoon completely."

"I've often wondered why she didn't take up woodwork as a career," Francie Wilford chipped in. "She has a real genius for it."

"Tom thinks of it as a hobby," Len said. "She wanted

much more than that for a lifework. If you ask me, she hit on the absolutely right thing."

"I agree," Aimée Robinet assented. "For Tom, her real work is a – a dedication – a vocation, in fact!"

They were silent a moment. The said Tom Gay had gone in for social work, especially social work with young boys. For the first twelve years of her life she had been brought up exactly like a boy and even now, for all her twenty-five years, she still retained many boyish tastes and ways of looking at things. Six years at the Chalet School had only modified them, and those of the girls who had seen her with her youngsters realized that she had found her right hole. She knew exactly how to handle her boys and was supremely happy and satisfied in every side of her work.

She trained them in woodwork, managed to find the right people to deal with those whose interests lay in other directions such as machinery, electricity, and other mechanical things, got up a subscription list which provided the Club she had helped to found with boats so that the boys might learn how to handle oars and sails, took them for long hikes into the country, established a library which contained the sort of yarns that are not included in the ordinary library catalogues but which appeal to schoolboys, and encouraged them to read and so come on to better work. In fact, she joined in all their interests as far as she was able. In return, she asked for loyalty to their Club, habits of regular washing and cleanliness, honesty in act and speech, and generosity in handing on their enjoyment to other boys.

Preaching she abominated, but most of the club members saw the example she set them and tried to follow it, even if only by fits and starts. And she did endless good. As one gentleman who went to inspect the Club and its activities remarked, "There are a good many small girls today who in later years should be thankful to Miss Gay for the husbands they've married!"

The girls' momentary silence was broken by the return of Maeve and Monica, bearing between them a wooden case, the lid of which had been levered open.

"We'll have to begin all over again!" Maeve gasped as they set their burden down. "Just look at this!"

They crowded round as she proceeded to take out other little houses and set them on the table.

"Heavens! Tom will be getting run in for exploiting child-labour!" Con cried. "She and those kids of hers must have toiled like ants! How many more, Maeve?"

"Fifteen, if you'll believe me! That makes forty-five all told. Here's a note that was on top. Shut up nattering and I'll read it."

In the ensuing silence, she read aloud, "Dear Maeve, I didn't know if we'd get this lot finished in time or not, but we've done it – with an almighty struggle. Hope they arrive in time. Mind you send me a detailed account of the show on Sunday or else expect trouble when we next meet. Good luck to it! Yours, Tom. P.S. Expect a shock in the near future!!!"

"And what she means by that, goodness only knows!" Maeve observed as she folded the note and slipped it into her pocket. "Well, we've got to begin all over again, so we'd better get down to it!"

The Seniors worked hard and by ten o'clock – 22.00 hours by mid-European time – the last doll was put in place and all that remained was for Gaudenz and his henchmen to spread tarpaulins over the show just in case it rained.

"Not that it looks like it," Len said, "but you never can tell!"

Next morning, at least half the school was up and out early. The mists were thinning on the Platz, though the valley beneath was still filled with a sea of opaque white. Far away, they could see the peaks of distant mountains which became clearer minute by minute. By the time they had had Frühstück, only a few wisps here and there remained and the sun blazed down, giving promise of another scorching day.

The girls rushed out to help remove the tarpaulins and give any finishing touches that were needed. The Sale itself began at 11.00 hours sharp and they had to change and be ready by 10.30 hours.

"Has the Countess arrived yet?" someone asked Len as, looking very Spanish in her black mantilla and huge green shawl, embroidered in flowers of every colour, she made her way to what they had unanimously named The Exhibition.

"I haven't a clue," Len said cheerfully. "It's not my pidgin, may I remind you, but the Head's, and I couldn't care less. You know, Primrose, I really do think this is Tom's chef-d'œuvre. But what did she mean when she said it made its own competition?"

"Goodness knows! Something hair-raising, you may be sure! How decent you look, Len! Quite Spanish, in spite of your red hair and fair skin. Now no one on earth could describe *me* that way!"

Len chuckled. "You might have dyed your hair and made up dark," she suggested wickedly.

"Yes; and can't you hear the Head on the subject when she saw me? I don't want to die just yet!" Primrose retorted.

Jane, looking, for all her fairness, far more Spanish than Primrose of the blue eyes, golden-brown locks and pink and white complexion, was standing near and giggled.

"*You're* all right," Primrose told her. "You look as if you'd walked out of Madrid with that white mantilla over the high comb and your lovely shawl. How have you managed it?"

"And how have you managed the earrings?" Len wanted to know.

"Tied them on with creamy embroidery silk." Jane lifted her mantilla to show.

"Brainy child! I never thought of that and as no one was likely to let me have my ears pierced for the occasion and I hate screws, I gave earrings a miss," Primrose said.

"Come on, you two!" called Maeve, appearing at that moment. "I want to make sure that we have enough pencils decently sharpened."

They went off and Jane moved over to the stall in charge of Upper IVA and B to admire it for about the fortieth time.

"I'd no idea we'd collected so much," she said to José who joined her. "Where *did* it all come from?"

"Oh, well, we all collected and after all there are – how many of us?" Twenty-five in our form – Hi, Ailie, how many in Lower IVA?"

"Twenty-four," said Ailie, shoving her straight-brimmed hat to such an angle that if it had not been secured by elastic at the back of her head, it would never have stayed on.

"Thanks! There you are, Jane! Forty-nine of us altogether. If we'd only produced two things each that would have been practically a hundred and lots of us got heaps more."

"I'm glad we got the bric-à-brac stall," Dilys observed. "I only hope we sell right out."

"I'm buying that string of Venetian beads for Mummy," José informed them. "She loves beads and those are really something."

"I want that big vase," Val Gardiner pointed to a wide terracotta affair. "We're rather missing on vases at Die Hütte and we're likely to be here for ages yet, so it would be awfully useful for flowers."

Jane looked eagerly at a letter-case in tooled Florentine leather. "I'd like that for Mother – and that tobacco-pouch for Father. They'd love them and those things would be easy to pack because they'd lie flat."

"If you people want to see Tom Gay's effort, come along now!" Margot Maynard had arrived in their midst. "Scram, all of you! There's no time to spare."

They rushed off to the screened corner where they were marshalled into line by Monica Garstin and Mary Murrell, two of the prefects who were on duty.

"In forms, please!" Mary said firmly. "Come along, Babies! Right in front!"

The last girl came panting up and then the screens were removed and they feasted their eyes on the Exhibition, exclaiming and admiring in half-a-dozen different languages. Not that they had long to look. Already visitors were to be seen coming up the road. The prefects slid the screen back into place and dismissed the girls to their stalls.

"Are you keeping the screens up?" demanded Prudence Dawbarn from VB.

"Of course we are," Rosamund told her.

"Why on earth?"

"Because people must pay to see it, of course," Ted Grantley grinned.

"What! Pay to see it and then pay again to enter for

it? I call that sharp practice! Still, it's all in a good cause," she added.

Five minutes later, Joey Maynard arrived in search of her daughters. They gaped at her open-mouthed when they saw her, for she was, to quote herself, in full regalia.

"Well! You certainly have got 'em all on!" Margot exclaimed.

"Haven't I?" Joey looked complacent. "Just for today, I'm Mrs Maynard, wife of the Head of the Sanatorium. Incidentally, I'm also the Lady Opener."

"But why?" Con gasped. "I thought the Comtesse Rambeau was that."

"So she was, but we had a 'phone-call this morning. The poor soul has been frantic with toothache the last two days and this morning, when she woke up, her face was so swollen she could scarcely open her mouth and certainly not open the Sale. They had to pitch on someone in a hurry. I'm the Victim!"

"Does Marie know?" Con queried. "She's been full of having her aunt here."

"Don't ask me; I haven't a clue! Stand still and let me look at you. Yes; you're really Spanish, Con; and Len isn't too bad either. You've had it Margot. It's an unfortunate choice where you're concerned. Anything *less* Spanish I've yet to behold!" Her eyes dwelt on Margot with her red-gold hair, blue eyes and milk-and-roses colouring.

"Wait till you see young Ailie!" Con grinned. "*She's* a mistake if you like!"

"She would be! Now let me go. I'm twittering with nerves. Opening sales isn't in my line at all and I haven't an idea what I'm going to say."

"You've never been at a loss yet," Len told her severely, "and you won't start at this late date. Only, I do beg of you, don't be *too* outrageous!"

"Impertinent hussy! I'm never outrageous. Here, you three! Here's a little something to strengthen your spending powers!" she handed them each a slim bundle of notes. "Where's my Felicity?"

"At the Wishing Well. She's a fairy." Len surveyed her mother again. "Oh, aren't we posh! A new hat and a new frock *and* your emeralds! You do look stately – not a bit like your usual self!"

"You just wait! Give this to Felicity and tell her to be ready for me at the Well." Joey handed her eldest another packet of notes and sauntered off at her most dignified.

On the way she met Jane, bringing an armful of paper carriers which Inter V had manufactured a few evenings before and then forgotten till the last minute. The Lady Opener paused.

"Well, Jane, how's life?"

"Oh, fabulous!" Jane's face lit up. "In his airmail, Father said that Mother was to be allowed to sit up in a chair for half an hour that day and when I go next week, I'll be with her every afternoon. Isn't it – " Jane paused for an appropriate adjective and fell back with a thud on "smashing!"

"Jane Carew! What an awful description! There – someone's yelling for you. Scram! I'll see you later!" And Joey went on, thinking that Jane was her old self once more.

By 11.00 hours, the grounds were swarming with people walking round, exclaiming at the quantity and variety of goods displayed and admiring the products of the art students in the way of Spanish houses and scenery. The school bell pealing out summoned them to the great front lawns. Joey, with her own husband as Chairman on one side, and the two Heads on the other, was introduced in proper form and proceeded to open the Sale in her own inimitable manner.

"As the first and oldest member of the Chalet School," she began, "I am delighted to welcome you to our Sale. I remember the first one we ever held – in the Dark Ages – and I remember," she looked wicked, "that during the preparations, I nearly slaughtered a member of staff by falling off a ladder and landing flat on her chest![1] I'll spare her blushes and not name her; but to relieve any anxiety you may feel about her, I should like to say that she is still with us and a most important leading member of the school."

She paused, perforce, silenced by the shouts of laughter and cheers from everyone who knew all about this episode, and smiled sweetly on Miss Wilson, who had given her a murderous glare. When silence fell, she went on.

"That Sale was a success. We were a very much smaller school in those days, but we handed over quite a sizeable contribution to the Sanatorium which was then on the Sonnalpe in Tirol. Since then, we have had one after another and I can honestly say that not one has been a flat failure. I know that everyone here will help us to keep up our record.

"I haven't heard that this has been preceded by any near-tragedy like the first, but I do know that just as we toiled to produce the most lavish articles we could manage, so have the girls of the present generation. And just as our visitors came that day, prepared to be generous, so, I'm sure, have you. We have two concerts to offer – one this morning and one in the afternoon. We have a play, written, produced and played by the girls themselves. There are several competitions to test your –

[1] *The Chalet School and the Lintons.*

ah – ingenuity. Our stalls are crammed with desirable articles of all kinds which should act as magnets to your purses. Finally, we have refreshments to offer those who feel faint on considering the amount they are spending. Please patronize everything at least once. You won't regret it. Apart from the return you get for your money, you will enjoy a happiness worth having when you think that you are helping to bring health and strength to many who might, otherwise, not know them.

"Right now I'm going to set you a good example. This may be a Spanish Sale, but I do beg all of you not to take the Spanish word 'Mañana' for your motto, but to *do it now!* Oh, I nearly forgot the most important thing I have to say. I declare this Sale open and wish it a howling success!" With which she left the daïs and made for the first stall, to the utter dismay of her own small Felicity, who had been chosen to present the customary bouquet, and the other folk who carried sprays or buttonholes for the rest of the people on the daïs, not to speak of the two doctors who should have proposed and seconded the votes of thanks.

Felicity was not to be disappointed, however. Clutching the big bouquet, she chased Joey, calling, "Mamma – Mamma! Come back and get your flowers!"

Joey stopped short, turned and accepted them with a kiss.

"Thank you, everyone," she said. "Felicity, run home, pet, and put them into water, will you? Then they'll have a chance to live. And now, let me see what I can spend, for I mean to go home with an empty purse. Everyone," she raised her voice. "Follow-my-leader! I'm going to *spend!*"

CHAPTER 20

Jane Looks Forward

"How much for this bowl, Jane? It's just what I want for bulbs."

Jane laughed. "80 francs – but isn't it too good for bulbs?"

Joey considered. "Perhaps you're right. I'll take it, all the same. Now what else have you people? José, I want two of those Indian bangles; and Jack, I'd like to look at those ash-trays, please. Yes; I'll take these two. Now what does all that come to – or can't you add it?" She grinned at them.

"It is 93 francs," Meg Walton said.

"Good!" Joey handed over a note for 100 francs. "Keep the change! This is an Occasion. Now I'm off to see how Tom has dealt with us." She pushed the parcels under the strawberry net fastened over the baby twins' pushchair, handed it over for safe-keeping to Con who was passing, and then made her way to the screened-off corner to tail on to a queue already waiting.

"Where are your purchases?" a friend demanded.

"Handed them over to Con. I'll retrieve them later. Hello! Here come the last lot of guessers. Frieda!" as a slight, fair woman came past. "Is the competition too awful?"

Frieda paused. "But terrible! I had no idea I had forgotten so much – er – well, you will see, Joey. Now I am going to Freudesheim to see how my baby is doing. But I will tell you," her eyes were full of mischief, "that you will be back in school again in a few minutes!" Then she sped off.

"Angels and ministers of Grace defend us!" Joey exclaimed. "This has no pleasant sound! What has that wretched Tom done now?"

Then she was paying Francie Wilford her entrance fee and gazing delightedly on The Exhibition.

"Oh, but this is wonderful!" she exclaimed. "Look at that lovely cottage! *And* the perfect little pagoda! There's an igloo – and *what* is that bird's-nest affair on sticks? This really is a triumph!"

Rikki Fry, in charge of the show, sounded a bell. "Everyone who wishes to enter for the competition please go round that screen," she said clearly.

Nearly everyone wished to enter and they went in single file round the screen, past another, and then found themselves entering a shed, usually dedicated to gardening tools, but now swept and garnished and furnished with another trestle table and forms all round it. Long slips of paper lay at every place with pencils on them and Maeve, in charge for this hour, requested everyone to sit down. When they were all seated, she spoke.

"First, you must promise to tell no one what you have to do," she said.

Everyone promised and Maeve continued, "Write your name at the top of the slip before you, *and* your full address. Then write down the names of the countries to which the little houses belong. The best list of all wins the prize. If anyone ties, there is another question to answer. You have seven minutes from – NOW!"

Everyone began scribbling for dear life, though presently some folk had to pause and think. It seemed almost no time before Maeve's voice rang out again. "Finish the word you are writing and then hand your slip to one of the people collecting them. Please go as soon as possible after that to make room for other people. Thank you!"

Aimée and Lizette collected the slips and passed them over to a small table behind the shed where a number of the two Sixths were hard at work checking them.

"Best list?" Mary Murrell demanded when they tossed the current ones into a box nearby. "Heather?"

"Mme Zetterling with twenty-three," Heather announced.

"Mme Mercier – twenty-seven," Betty Landon followed quickly.

"Mme Charlot has just eighteen," Rosamund Lilley said sadly.

"I do not blame her," Suzanne Kiefen remarked. "It is a terrible competition."

"Trust Tom!" Margot finished counting up. "Mum comes out of it better. Thirty-seven for her."

Meanwhile, the people in the play had been summoned to get something to eat before they went to dress and make up. About eight people from Lower IVA and Upper IVB who were selling programmes went with them.

"Feeling wonky, Jane?" Jack asked as she passed Jane the sugar.

"Butterflies in the tummy," Jane said dismally. "I can't eat another thing."

"Of course you can! Go on!" Jack urged her. "You don't want to do a flop in the middle of the show, do you? Well, then!"

Jane sighed. "I know it sounds mad to you, but I honestly feel all dithery."

"I don't see why. You've done it before." Jack was puzzled.

"I know. It just doesn't make any difference."

"But you won't go *on* feeling like that every time will you? You said you meant to go on the stage," José said.

"I know. And I do – I wouldn't do anything else."

"But if you feel bad before every show, why not choose something else?" forthright Jack demanded. "It isn't worth it!"

"Oh, but it is!" Jane spoke earnestly. "I couldn't possibly do anything else!"

"Well, I don't understand. It sounds quite mad to me."

Jane bolted her last spoonful of apricots and cream. "I expect it does, but there it is. What's more, Jack, I've heard Mother say she felt the same, but she couldn't bear to give it up. And once you begin, it goes."

"Jane – *Jane!* Stop nattering with Jack and come on! You haven't any too much time, you know!"

Jane jumped up and fled, leaving Jack to ponder on the queerness of choosing a job that made you feel like that, before she also departed to seek her programmes and bag of change. She had been delighted to be one of the chosen, for the Head had decreed that as the school had already seen the play, only the usherettes could be present this time. How wise she had been in laying down this law was seen when every chair in Hall was filled five minutes before the curtain went up, even the stools down the sides meant for the usherettes being occupied, while those young persons had to content themselves with the windowsills.

It was a success – no doubt of that. All the players were much better and Jane, all her flutters forgotten, was, as Jack remarked, "*Germaine* and nobody else!" When it ended and the entire cast had taken their bow, it was Jack who set up a yell of, "*Germaine – Germaine! We want Germaine!*"

The rest of the Junior Middles band took it up and the

visitors joined in. Jane had to appear before the curtains and curtsy her thanks not once, but three times before they let her go. It ended at last and while the visitors streamed away to seek iced lemonade, fruit drinks, ices and other refreshments, the actors hurriedly changed back into Spanish costume and then went to see how the stalls had got on during their absence. All had a very denuded look.

"Mean to say that's all we've got left?" demanded Jack, who had waited for Jane with José and Wanda.

Jean nodded happily. "Nearly everything's gone. But we took your things out, you people, and shoved them into that box and they're all safe. Dilys, haven't you folk finished counting that cash yet?'

"Nearly," Dilys said, raising a flushed face. "How much have you got there, Kitty? And you, Sally? Here, write it down under here. Now I'll add it up."

She added it three times, slowly and carefully, with the others to check her. Finally she looked up with eyes almost ready to drop out.

"You'll never believe it, but we've made nearly 2,000 francs – well, 1,947 to be accurate!"

Jack whistled. "I *say!* That's smashing! Up the Fourths!"

"Of course," Jean said as detachedly as she could, "we did have those lovely Florentine leather things your mother sent us, Sancia; and then there were the wood carvings your father and brothers did for us, Marta. They brought in quite a sum. And there was that lovely bowl Mrs Maynard bought from you, Jane. Still, even the little things have sold. It's not half-bad, is it?"

Jack was looking round. "Pity we haven't sold everything," she remarked. "I've got 7 francs left. What's the price of that bracket?"

"Ten – but you can have it for seven," Barbara Hewlett said. "I'm spent up, but there's this notebook with painted covers for 3 francs and the little polished wood box at 5 francs and these odd postcards if anyone would like to have them."

Fired by Jack's example, they rushed to buy and when some of the prefects came along to see how they had done, it was with righteous pride that they announced, "Sold out completely!"

"What happens next?" Jane asked José.

"Draws and competition results. Got your tickets? Come on, then. There's the bell!"

"You and Jean take that money to Deney in the office," said Prudence Dawbarn behind them. "She's there, collecting. Don't forget to write your total on a slip to go with it. Scram! The draws are beginning!"

Jean and Barbara gathered up the money and the slip Dilys had printed to go with it, and raced off to hand it over to Miss Dene before tearing back to join the others. A good many people had left by this time, but there was still quite a crowd standing about listening to the results of the draws. José whispered to the two form prefects that a big box of chocolates had been won by someone staying at one of the pensions on the Platz, and a copper bowl had gone to some other stranger.

"But Mlle de Lachennais has won those gorgeous embroidered lawn hankies, and that kid Felicity Maynard won the afternoon tea-set Lady Russell sent," José told them. "This is for the tea-cloth Sybil Russell made."

To the delight of the girls, it went to Nancy Wilmot, and the next draw, a charming water-colour, fell to Miss Wilson. There were two or three more and then came the competitions. Frau Mieders' huge iced cake was won by Aimée Robinet's mother and she promptly presented it to the School amid cheers and clapping from the girls. Con Maynard had guessed the name – "Solange' – of a big doll dressed as a Breton fisher-girl, and put it in her little sister's arms as she came away with it. Jack had a pretty brooch for hammering nails into a plank and Maeve won a silver vase for a smelling competition. Adrienne got a tennis racquet for tossing the greatest number of ping-pong balls into a bucket. With most folk, the things bounced out again, but Adrienne seemed to have a knack for it.

Young Dr Gordon walked off with a box of six golfballs for the clock golf, and Len Maynard and Rosamund Lilley came forward to claim the prize for guessing the most book titles and retired each with a handsome copy of one of Thackeray's novels. And so it went on until at last there was only Tom Gay's Exhibition to be won. There was quite a stir when Dr Jack handed his wife a sealed envelope which she opened so deliberately that one or two small people danced with impatience. However, she took out the slip bearing the name of the winner at long last and stared incredulously at it.

"Well, crisp me in a frying-pan!" she exclaimed, her clear tones reaching to every corner of the garden. "Believe it or not, I've won it!" She stopped short and looked severely at the assembled school. "Do you girls mean to tell me that I, who left school more years ago than I care to remember, have beaten you who are still *at* school?"

Peals of laughter broke out, but she held up her hand for silence.

"I can only say I'm horrified! In fact, I think the only thing to do is to present this prize to the geography room in the hopes that before long all of you will be able to recognize a pagoda when you see it and also an African pigmy's tree-nest. Miss Annersley," she turned to the Head who was stifling her laughter with difficulty, "I have much pleasure in making this presentation where I feel it will do most good."

Miss Annersley replied in a choked voice, "Th-thank you!"

But it was no use. She broke off and rocked with mirth while Joey, still as grave as a judge, gazed at her with wide eyes. The girls joined in the laughter and it was only finally hushed when someone – most people thought it was Jack, but she always denied it furiously – called for three cheers for Mrs Maynard. They were given, but a good many folk were short of breath by this time.

That ended the Sale so far as the visitors were concerned. They departed, and at last only the school and the Sanatorium representatives remained.

"And now," said the Head, "Abendessen! I'm sure we all need it. After that, we'll go into Hall for a grand tally and you shall hear how we've done this year. School, go and wash and tidy!" She smiled at the small group of doctors and nurses as the School obeyed. "If anyone else would like to do likewise, there is a cloakroom in my annexe and a bathroom above it. Some of the mistresses will be delighted to show you the way, I know." She turned to Joey. "You're staying, Joey. Anna asked me to tell you that she will put the babies to bed, so there is no need for you to go home."

"Oh yes, there is!" Joey retorted. "I'm going to change into something old and comfortable and attend to my hands and face. But I'll be back shortly, so don't eat up all the best! I know Karen's special feasts!"

She fled on the last word, but was back ten minutes later, attired in an old cotton frock, her hair smooth and shining, and looking, as she said she felt, herself once more.

"I like pretty clothes," she said as she enjoyed Karen's iced bouillon, "but I never feel like myself in new clothes. Oh, that was good! What comes next?"

Finally, they all adjourned to Hall, where the girls sank happily into the deckchairs they had brought with them while the Staff, the doctors and nurses and Joey congregated on the dais and counted up the takings. It was a lengthy business, but at last Jack Maynard stood up amid an excited buzz and beamed on everyone.

"Congratulations, School! You've made exactly 1,563 francs 55 centimes more than last year, and this means that at long last we can make a beginning on the new children's ward we need so badly. And since it is owing to this magnificent sum that we *can* begin now, we are gong to call it The Chalet School Ward. Thank you very much, one and all, both for myself and also on behalf of every single person connected with the Sanatorium. Bless you!"

He sat down and the School broke loose. They did just leave the roof on, but Miss Wilson vowed that it was only by a miracle. Some people embraced their nearest neighbours. Maeve danced an Irish jig. Jack and Jane, happening to be next to each other, caught hands and swung madly round and round till Miss Wilmot firmly parted them and sat them down in the nearest chairs.

When the Maynards finally left to go home, they encountered the pair strolling along the path to Freudesheim, talking hard. Joey stopped.

"Well, Jane, the term is nearly over – your first term at any school. How has it been?"

Jane raised eyes glowing with happiness. "Oh, *darling!*" she cried. "It's been stupendous! I'm longing to see

Mother and Father again and I know I'll have a lovely holiday in Sydney. But just the same, I'll be looking forward to next term and another glorious time at the Chalet School!"

Armada
Gift Classics

An attractive collection of beautifully illustrated stories, including some of the finest and most enjoyable children's stories ever written.

Some of the older, longer titles have been skilfully edited and abridged.

Little Women	*Louisa M. Alcott*	£2.25 ☐
Peter Pan	*J. M. Barrie*	£2.25 ☐
The Wizard of Oz	*L. Frank Baum*	£1.95 ☐
Lorna Doone	*R. D. Blackmore*	£1.95 ☐
What Katy Did	*Susan M. Coolidge*	£2.25 ☐
What Katy Did at School	*Susan M. Coolidge*	£1.95 ☐
What Katy Did Next	*Susan M. Coolidge*	£1.95 ☐
The Wind in the Willows	*Kenneth Grahame*	£2.25 ☐
The Secret Garden	*Frances Hodgson Burnett*	£2.25 ☐
The Phantom of the Opera	*Gaston Leroux*	£1.95 ☐
The Railway Children	*E. Nesbit*	£1.95 ☐
The Scarlet Pimpernel	*Baroness Orczy*	£1.95 ☐
Black Beauty	*Anna Sewell*	£1.95 ☐
Kidnapped	*R. L. Stevenson*	£1.95 ☐
Treasure Island	*R. L. Stevenson*	£1.95 ☐
Dracula	*Bram Stoker*	£1.95 ☐
Gulliver's Travels	*Jonathan Swift*	£1.95 ☐
The Adventures of Tom Sawyer	*Mark Twain*	£1.95 ☐
Around the World in 80 Days	*Jules Verne*	£2.25 ☐

ARMADA

No Chalet School collection
will be complete without

Elinor M. Brent-Dyer's Chalet School

*by Elinor M. Brent-Dyer
and Helen McClelland*

Elinor M. Brent-Dyer's famous Chalet School series, begun in 1925, is still as popular as ever – and this fascinating compendium of Chalet School facts is a must for Chalet School fans of any age.

Included are:

★ **Articles about the history of the school and its main characters**

★ **Information about the mysterious Miss Brent-Dyer**

★ **Two short stories, unpublished since the 1940s**

★ **Quizzes**

★ **Competitions**

Find out about the ideas behind these delightful stories, only available in Armada.

£3.99 ☐

ARMADA

Run With the Hare

LINDA NEWBERY

A sensitive and authentic novel exploring the workings of an animal rights group, through the eyes of Elaine, a sixth-form pupil. Elaine becomes involved with the group through her more forceful friend Kate, and soon becomes involved with Mark, an Adult Education student and one of the more sophisticated members of the group. Elaine finds herself painting slogans and sabotaging a fox hunt. Then she and her friends uncover a dog fighting ring – and things turn very nasty.

£2.50 ☐

Hairline Cracks

JOHN ROBERT TAYLOR

A gritty, tense and fast-paced story of kidnapping, fraud and cover ups. Sam Lydney's mother knows too much. She's realized that a public inquiry into the safety of a nuclear power station has been rigged. Now she's disappeared and Sam's sure she has been kidnapped, he can trust no one except his resourceful friend Mo, and together they are determined to uncover the crooks' operation and, more importantly, find Sam's mother.

£2.50 ☐

ARMADA

The Three Investigators
Series

Meet the Three Investigators – brilliant Jupiter Jones, athletic Pete Crenshaw and studious Bob Andrews. Their motto, "We investigate anything" has led them into some bizarre and dangerous situations. Join the three boys in their sensational mysteries, available only in Armada.

ARMADA

The Chalet School
Series

ELINOR M. BRENT-DYER

Elinor M. Brent-Dyer has written many books about life at the famous alpine school. Follow the thrilling adventures of Joey, Mary-Lou and all the other well-loved characters in these delightful stories, available only in Armada.

ARMADA

All these books are available at your local bookshop or newsagent, or can be ordered from the publisher. To order direct from the publishers just tick the title you want and fill in the form below:

Name _____

Address _____

_____

Send to: Collins Childrens Cash Sales
          PO Box 11
          Falmouth
          Cornwall
          TR10 9EN

Please enclose a cheque or postal order or debit my Visa/ Access –

   Credit card no:

   Expiry date:

   Signature:

– to the value of the cover price plus:

UK: 80p for the first book and 20p per copy for each additional book ordered to a maximum charge of £2.00.

BFPO: 80p for the first book and 20p per copy for each additional book.

Overseas and Eire: £1.50 for the first book, £1.00 for the second book. Thereafter 30p per book.

Armada reserve the right to show new retail prices on covers which may differ from those previously advertised in the text or elswhere.

ARMADA